KINGS
OF THE
Castle

Book 1- Introduction to the Series

Books 2 - 9 are Standalones

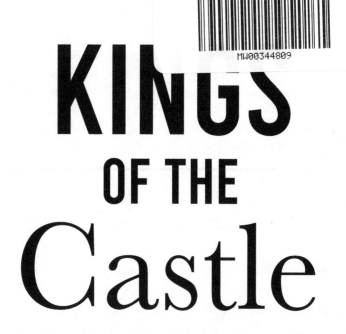

Naleighna Kai
S. L. Jennings
J. L. Campbell
Martha Kennerson
Lisa Watson
Karen D. Bradley
Janice M. Allen
London St. Charles
and MarZe Scott

Macro Publishing Group
Chicago, Illinois

This is a work of fiction. All characters and events in this book are purely fictitious, a creation of the author's imagination and any resemblance to actual persons, living or dead, or somewhere in between is coincidental.

Kings of the Castle - Book 1 of the Kings of the Castle Series
Books 2-9 are standalone books.

Published by:
Macro Publishing Group
1507 E. 53rd Street, Suite 858
Chicago, Illinois
www.thekingsofthecastle.com

Trade Paperback ISBN: 978-1-7331782-1-1
Digital ISBN: 978-1-7331782-0-4

Cover Design by: Woodson Creative Studio
www.woodsoncreativestudio.com

Interior Design by: Lissa Woodson
www.naleighnakai.com

KINGS
OF THE
Castle

Book 1 - Introduction to the series

Books 2 - 9 are standalone books

♦ DEDICATION ♦

Kassanna Dwight and LaVerne Thompson. Women who kept the faith when everyone else had doubts. Enjoyed meeting you at the CrossRoads.

♦ ACKNOWLEDGEMENTS ♦

First to the Creator from whom all blessings flow. To NK's Tribe Called Success, we thank you.

Kassana, LaVerne Thompson, Ursuala Sinclair, Jenetta M. Bradley, Sesvalah, Katara Johnson, (KOC's Personal Assistant), Dee VPA, Olivia Gaines, Simone Choi, Siera London, Angela Kay Austin, Areana Jones, Bobby Kim, Mary Green, and Radiah Hubbert.

To our editors Janice M. Allen, Brynn Weimer, and Mo Sytsma—thanks for the red ink and everything you all did to make this a smoother and awesome book.

To our beta readers Crystal Baltimore, Debra J. Mitchell, Dani Sibley, and Brynn Weimer, we appreciate your efforts.

A special thanks to J. L. Woodson for this dynamic cover, and the covers for the entire series. Much love, young man.

To the rest of our NK Tribe Called Success family: J. D. Mason, Pat G'Orge-Walker, Anita L. Roseboro, Sierra Kay, Shakir Rashaan, Michelle D. Rayford, and Terri Ann Johnson.

To our InScribe team, Kelly Peterson, Mallori—you are the absolute best. Mark Jackson, thank you for the awesome trailer.

Finally, thank you to everyone who purchased this book and our efforts. Your support is greatly appreciated.

Many thanks to the Kings of the Castle Amabassadors who supported the series ...

Adrenna Shipman, Amanda McCoy, Amber Dowell, Angela Sims, Anita L. Roseboro, Areana Senoj, Arlene Reynolds, B Fly Brooks, Brenda Pious, Bryn Drescher, Brynn Weimer, Cara Boyce, **Cassandra Haywood**, Cheryl Forbes Montgomery, **Christine Pauls, Crystal A. Baltimore, Dani Sibley,** Darline Marsh, Debra J. Mitchell, Dee Washington, Deitriah Reese, DeJuan Mason, Desna Jackson, Ebony Danille Goodrich, Ebony Walker, **Ellen Kiley Goeckler**, Ellowyn Young Bell, Felecia Thompson Peeples, Flo Brooks, Gail Diamond, Georgiana Braham, Glomika Taylor, Goldy Gaines, Jr., Helen Ross, Jackie Roberts, Jackson Michelle, Jacqueline L. Armor, Jeanelle Poole-Blanchard, Jenetta Bradley, Jennifer Cole Addison, Jennifer Fraser, Joelle Adams, Johnson Monica Anderson, Johnnetta Godbee, Joyce M. Hudson, Juanita Lee Samms, Julia Landry, Karen Williams, Kassanna, Katara Johnson, Kathleen Jones Bass, Kathryn Davis, Katie Walsh Giannini, Kendra Denise, Keturah Newton, Kisha Green, LaCeasha Banks Turner, LaTanya Wright, Latisha Dewalt, LaVerne Thompson, Lennie Morris, Leslie Dishman, Linda Cureton, Linda Miller, Lisa Watson, Lora Nance Davis, Lori Hays, Lulu Dudley, Marilyn Diamond, Marilyn Gerber, Marsharee Danielle Rocker-Austin, Marva Harden, **MeMe Rogers**, Michelle D. Jackson, Michelle D. Rayford, Michelle Marshall, Nicole Wolfe, Olesa Taylor, Olivia Gaines, **Pat G'Orge Walker**, Patrice Ball Reed, Patricia Johnson, Patricia Raspberry, Phoenix Ash, Rebecca Lewis, Rebecca Rodgers, Regina Elise, Rhonda Crosby, Robi Lynn Lewis, Rochelle Dodd, Ronni Roseman, Rosalyn Lewis, Ruth Jones Johnson, Ruth Russell Hutton, Sally Marsh, Samantha

Woods Wynton, **Shae Cross**, Shakir Rashaan, Sharon Chinn Vance, Sharon Eatmon-Roland, Shavonna Futrell, Shea Brown, Shunda Yates, Sierra Kay, Sonia White-Lowery, Stacey White, Taija Woods, Tandria Jones, Tangra Lavett, Terri Johnson, Tica Fields, **Tiffany Finley**, **Tina Miller-Drew, Toni Coleman Scruggs**, Tonya Anderson Holmes, Unique Hiram, Valerie Thomas Smith, Vernon Gaines, Victoria Adams-Kennedy, Viktoria Niecey Roberts, Wanda Dixon, and Yaya McIntyre.

ABOUT THE KINGS OF THE CASTLE SERIES

Books 2-9 are standalones, no cliffhangers, and can be read in any order.

Book 1 – Kings of the Castle, the introduction to the series and story of King of Wilmette (Vikkas Germaine)

USA TODAY, *New York Times*, and National Bestselling Authors work together to provide you with a world you'll never want to leave. The Castle. Powerful men unexpectedly brought together by their pasts and current circumstances will become a force to be reckoned with. Their combined efforts to find the people responsible for the attempt on their mentor's life, is the beginning of dangerous challenges that will alter the path of their lives forever. Not to mention, they will also draw the ire and deadly intent of current Castle members who wield major influence across the globe.

Fate made them brothers, but protecting the Castle and the women they love, will make them Kings.

www.thekingsofthecastle.com

King of Chatham - Book 2 - Reno
King of Evanston - Book 3 - Shaz
King of Devon - Book 4 - Jai
King of Morgan Park - Book 5 - Daron
King of South Shore - Book 6 - Kaleb
King of Lincoln Park - Book 7 - Grant
King of Hyde Park - Book 8 - Dro
King of Lawndale - Book 9 - Dwayne

CHAPTER 1

JAIDEV MAHARAJ

"What do you mean she's pregnant?" Jai roared. "She's been in a coma ever since she arrived."

He paced the length of his office and held his tongue. Several emotions fought for dominance and his assistant, Kelly, who had brought such horrific news, didn't deserve his vocalized rage. The one emotion that overpowered all others was anger.

A young woman who arrived at Chetan Health Center after a horrific highway accident a year ago, was now nearly seven months pregnant. No one—not staff, nor the doctors, nor any of the people he had hired—were aware of the pregnancy. The center was wired with a state-of-the-art surveillance system. How had someone managed to violate a woman this way?

Jai took a long slow breath, exhaled, then whispered, "So, I'm supposed to believe that one of our male employees impregnated a comatose patient in our care?"

Kelly averted her gaze, taking a pointed interest in the abstract artwork on the walls of his modestly furnished office. "We don't have any idea who it was."

"You know this has to be reported immediately," he said. A sinking feeling lodged in the pit of his belly. "Call in the police, our lawyers, and put all of the male employees in the conference room. I need to give them a heads up."

Jai agonized over the undeniable violation. A comatose woman? How vile. But the obvious sign that something had happened was there. She was carrying a child.

Kelly placed the call, keyed something into her cell, then blinked, frowning as her green eyes scanned the screen. "Do you know a Khalil Germaine?"

Khalil Germaine, his mentor and teacher from the time Jai had attended Macro International Magnet School. A man who had made a positive impact on his life and was the main reason he had chosen a career in holistic medicine. "He was like a father to me, but what does that have to do with what's happening right now?"

"I just received a text from the front desk," she replied, turning her screen to face Jai. "His son called and asked for you to come right away. He's been shot, and they have him in ICU."

Jai stood frozen in the center of his office, and a new set of emotions filtered through him—guilt, pain, sadness. Khalil had made several attempts at getting Jai to accept something he called becoming a King of The Castle.

The Castle had been a sprawling estate with Moroccan style stone buildings, reminiscent of old World England with an African flair. It had been a place where wealthy people indulged any and everything their hearts desired. Only a small percentage of that had a sexual slant. Accepting Khalil's invitation to join an organization called The Castle would have taken more bandwidth than Jai had to give. Now he wondered if he had been wrong to dismiss the requests so quickly.

Jai finally found his bearings, but Kelly, who had kept her focus on him for those several moments, chimed in. "If it's who I think it is, then that's considered family business. I can handle things here." She moved her hands in a shooing motion. "Go."

He grabbed his briefcase from one of the leather chairs, saying, "Call me the minute—"

"Got it. Go!"

He stopped at the door and glanced at her over his shoulder. "First, I think I need to address the men who work here. They're about to be hit with all kinds of madness and I want them to be prepared."

"Sounds fair," she whispered, then gestured toward the hallway.

Jai was out the door in a flash.

CHAPTER 2

DARON KINCAID

The words *my daughter is missing* broke through Daron's sleep haze.

He bolted from the bed, glanced at the clock, his heart racing at what Katara Johnson—one of his few remaining clients—had just spoken over the phone. He whispered, "Is her tracker working?"

"It showed movement until forty-five minutes ago." Katara's soft voice was choppy with a crackling noise that overlaid every other word.

The emergency tracking device, a pair of diamond studs, was one of the items he had developed as a personal security gadget for single ladies. Most people would never think a woman's earrings could be so functional. Daron designed it so all a woman had to do was press the earring to alert her listed contacts and activate the tracking system. If someone had her tied up, she could easily use a shoulder to press her ear to activate it.

Katara continued, "I gave the police the last location. They didn't arrive in time, but they located her cell."

"We'll find her." He flipped back the satin sheet, noting the rise and fall of Cameron's chest as he slid out the bed, wondering if he should alert her to the situation. When an earlier text notification about unexpected gunfire at The Castle required that he send several men from his former operations team to contain the situation, he definitely hadn't tipped her off to that incident. He slipped on his discarded boxer briefs, grabbed a pair of jogging pants off the chaise, and threw them over his shoulder.

With his hand, he used the edge of the mattress to guide him closer to the door so that he wouldn't disturb his sleeping beauty. The glow from his phone helped him find the knob and he entered the hall. The light came on immediately as he moved across the wood planks and turned off as he cleared the area.

"I can drive to the last location we had before losing the signal," Katara offered.

"You don't need to." He trotted down the stairs to the basement. The polished cement was cool underneath his bare feet as he slid behind the bar. "Give me a minute to log in to the system."

"I can't lose her," she sobbed.

"Let's focus on finding her and quickly." He entered the multi-level storage area behind the bar, moving cases of beer so that he could access his workspace. The steel door swung open.

"My phone was in my locker and my mom's phone died. I didn't realize until …" She began crying uncontrollably.

Daron focused, keyed in the information, trying not to let her panic affect him. He placed two fingers on the touch screen monitor on the wall, pressing the areas near the flashing dot before spreading them apart to zoom in. "Katara. Katara," he said, then waited until she quieted enough to hear him. "My people should be receiving a new location. I'll send you an update if the location changes."

Katara sniffled. "I got it."

"Call me back when you have her." Daron disconnected the call, hoping that they'd make it to the girl in time and also praying she was alive and hadn't been physically or sexually assaulted. So much was happening in Chicago right now.

He slipped on a pair of jogging pants, wishing he'd snatched up a shirt. Tracy had been out of contact for twelve hours. He wanted to be more hands-on with the search, but he was probably of better use where he was stationed.

When he promised Cameron that he would open a legitimate firm that provided security systems, he meant every word. For the last few years Daron, under the street moniker, The Warden, had been the brains behind an illegal organization. The sole purpose was to take down Chase Prescott's family business from the inside. The repercussions of helping a task force put an international crime ring behind bars still lingered, and had become the main source of contention in his budding relationship with Cameron. He had made a promise that no more of the "cloak and dagger" lifestyle would shadow them. That was fast becoming a promise he couldn't keep.

* * *

Daron felt like he'd spent hours staring at the green blinking dot and glancing at his phone but it had only been forty-five minutes. The dot was on the move. He didn't know if that was a good thing or not. He tried not to imagine all the scenarios that could be happening, but had to wait until the dot remained in one area before he could give anyone an update on the location.

When he developed the tracking system, Daron wanted to help combat sex trafficking and protect women who tended to be alone a great deal of the time. He hadn't given any thought to the problems that could arise for him when the actions that needed to be taken brought him close to anything that resembled his old life.

His thoughts shifted to Cameron, asleep upstairs, who felt like family even though they had only been dating a few months. Except for the few nights she was with him, she was, despite her personal safety measures, going home alone all times of night depending on her hectic schedule. While she was skilled in martial arts and her weapons collection was ridiculous, it didn't stop Daron from worrying that someone would catch her off guard, or use someone close to her to set a trap and take her from him. She still had a lot of enemies thanks to her former criminal mastermind boss, Bishop, where she had been a weapon of choice for most jobs from stealing multi-million-dollar art and sculptures to assignments that put fear into his competition.

While she had taken steps to distance herself from everything on the wrong side of the law, Daron had created a program for young men and wanted to do something to help bring missing girls home. Now, as the minutes ticked by, he didn't know if the tracking device was the right solution. Secrecy was the key. Unfortunately, the more devices he sold meant more chances of the word getting out. The traffickers would make sure the earrings were off before moving their victims.

The idea of not being able to bring Tracy home to Katara pained him. So many Black and Brown girls were going missing without a trace in this age of technology and high-performance cameras. The few that were found weren't always alive.

Two hours later, he expanded the screen. The dot's speed had changed. It now seemed to be lingering in one small space.

Daron locked in the location, sent the coordinates to his awaiting team. Twenty minutes later, his cell chimed. Glancing down, the words 'The Castle' flashed back. He reached for it just as a call came through.

"We have Tracy," Katara said, and the happiness in her voice warmed his heart.

His head dipped forward in relief. "How is she?"

"In shock. A little bruised and drugged up, but she and the other girls are safe now."

Other girls?

Katara paused, giving someone else a directive before coming back on the line. "Thank you so much. I gotta go. Bye."

Two high-alert events in one night could not be a coincidence.

CHAPTER 3

VICTOR ALEJANDRO "DRO" REYES

"Don't disgrace your family, hijo."

"Shouldn't you be telling that to Uncle Santiago, Mamá?"

Dro sat on the bench of his grand piano. The dimly lit conservatory echoed his dark mood. His fingers moved skillfully across the keys. Beethoven's Piano Sonata No. 8 in C minor, Op. 13, commonly known as Sonata Pathétique, resounded through the far reaches of the room. The composition was one of his mother's favorites, and after the disagreement he'd had with her hours before, he needed a distraction. Music always served a vital purpose.

"Sir?"

"Not now, Travers," Dro called over his shoulder.

"But, you have an important phone call," Nicholas Travers replied.

"Take a message, please." He returned to his playing while Travers disappeared as quickly as he'd come.

Dro's day had been a long and stressful one. Right now, he wanted a few moments of reprieve. The heated conversation he'd had with the first love of his life, Valentina Aragón Reyes, was a doozy. He'd tried to avoid it, but his mother wouldn't let up. Uncle Santiago had contacted him repeatedly over the last few days. Too busy with his current assignment, Dro had put off returning the calls. He knew what his uncle wanted. A favor here, a word of introduction there, his uncle took family favors to another level, almost as far as his mother took her guilt trips.

His father, Victor, had overlooked this flaw in his baby brother. But considering that he, too, was the baby of the family, Dro had little patience for his uncle's weaknesses. The irony was that Victor Reyes had always hammered into his children the importance of being successful, of using the brains God gave them, and of always putting family first. Santiago had received the same wisdom from his father as a child, but somehow, it hadn't stuck. His business acumen, or lack thereof, was legendary in their family. By squandering nearly every opportunity that came his way, Santiago had become their grandfather's biggest disappointment and his father's burden. And now he was Dro's burden.

"I'm sorry to disturb you again," Travers said.

"But?" Dro sighed. His fingers froze, hovering in mid-air over the ivory piano keys.

"It's your office line again. Ellen Kiley is insistent, sir."

Dro stood, abandoning all hope of letting that sonata carry him into a peaceful mood. As he walked past, he patted Travers on the shoulder. "Thanks so much."

He walked down the hall from the conservatory to his office. His quick stride beat out a steady cadence on the hardwood floors. The light was already on at his desk, and the hold button was blinking steadily on the telephone. Picking up the receiver, Dro dropped into a chair near the window that provided a view of his lush gardens and retrieved the call.

"What's up, El?"

"Sorry to call you at this hour, Mr. Reyes," his assistant of seven years replied.

"Dro," he instantly corrected. A friend of his mother's, Ellen had insisted on being more formal in the office. When she didn't reply, his chest rumbled with laughter. "It's no problem. Travers said you needed me?"

"You received a call a few minutes ago—on your private line."

The teasing stopped. After hours, Dro's private line rolled to Natalie, and if she didn't answer, then it went to his cell. He knew if someone was calling on that line, it was an issue that was a high priority.

"Let's have it."

"Alderman Cherry needs to speak with you. Immediately."

His gaze flicked to his watch. Almost midnight, but if the alderman had reached out to him this late, this wasn't a social call.

"Thanks, El. Goodnight."

"Goodnight, sir."

Switching to his cell, he dialed the alderman's number and waited. The man picked up on the first ring.

"Hi Sam," Dro said casually. "How can I be of service?"

"I forgot you always get to the point. I need a favor."

All business, Dro grabbed a pen and notepad from the far end of the cherry wood desk and asked, "What do you need?"

Sam was silent for a few moments before he said, "It's Nina. She's … she's in trouble," he replied gruffly. "She left hours ago to go to her friend's house. Supposedly to a party, but that was a lie."

Dro jotted down notes.

"She and one of her schoolmates went to some hotel. They weren't alone," he stressed. "Another friend received a few text messages from my baby, along with some pictures. She wisely told her mother about it, and the mother called my wife."

Dro could hear the man struggling to hold it together. His voice cracked when he said, "Nina needs help, but I don't know where she is. Just that she's in a hotel and was given something. If they harm a hair on her—"

"I need you to focus, Sam," Dro replied. "If I'm to help, I need all the facts right now."

Sam repeated all the information his wife, June, had relayed. He gave Dro the cell numbers of his daughter and her friend.

"Dro—"

"I know, Sam. This situation has to stay under the radar. I'll handle it."

Sam let out a sigh of relief.

"Thank you."

The moment he disconnected, Dro called Ellen back and brought her up to speed.

"Get Mike on this. I need to know where she is, what's been posted on social media—"

"From her cell, and her girlfriend's phone in the last few hours," Ellen added.

He rattled off a few more orders before ending the call. Sam was an advocate for members of The Castle. So without question, he would get whatever he needed.

After his father's illness and sudden retirement, Dro was in line to inherit his seat as one of Chicago's Kings of the Castle. He was reluctant to step into the role, but his brothers, Raul and Esteban said they would flat out refuse if asked. Not wanting to hurt their father, and because it was his nature, Dro decided he would accept if offered. The position was a full-time engagement, and the only way out is to step down due to health issues that prohibited anyone from doing the job, inheritance, or by death. Dro was well aware of the perks, prestige, danger, and commitment of being a King. They had limitless connections across the globe, most of whom were loyal to the Kings of the Castle, but from what he had learned recently, they also had major enemies. He'd gone over everything in his head from the day his father made the request. He was a Reyes. He would accept his father's seat. Dro had no regrets.

The next call he placed was to his good friend, Shastra "Shaz" Bostwick, who had worked with him on several occasions.

When their conversation ended ten minutes later, he rushed upstairs to his bedroom to change. His family issues were forgotten and a few thoughts of how far he'd have to go to solve Alderman Cherry's problem came to mind.

Dro had a job to do, and it was time to go to work.

CHAPTER 4

SHAZ BOSTWICK

Camilla Gibson's eyes were deep enough for Shaz to lose himself in them. Someone in her position shouldn't have been this demanding, but he understood. Camilla was clutching at straws to save her baby. If he were a parent, he'd be doing the same thing.

He dragged his gaze from hers and let it settle on the ocean painting on the wall across from him. A heavy mahogany desk and Queen Anne chairs should have made his workspace austere, but the egg-shell blue walls, corner sofa, and potted plants gave his office a warm atmosphere and made his clients comfortable.

Now that he'd regained his bearings, Shaz studied the woman who had walked in for an early appointment and brought back painful memories from his past. Her brown eyes carried deep shadows that hinted at the torment wracking her soul. She shifted, and he put aside thoughts of family and separation.

"Can you help me, or not?" she asked, as her eyes lasered into his.

Camilla's hair fell in soft, chestnut waves around her head, and with one hand, she pushed several strands of it off her forehead. She grimaced, and he didn't know if she was hurting or annoyed with him. He pulled his mind back from the unexpected desire to thread the thick strands of her hair through his fingers. Instead, he rolled one of his locs to occupy his hand.

The phone rang, and he was grateful for the distraction. Camilla had thrown him off-kilter, and he didn't like it one bit. She was as mouth-watering as the food her aunt served at the Jamaican restaurant down the street. Shaz made it a point to eat at Miss Mabel's at least once each week. The food carried a home-cooked flavor that was reminiscent of his childhood summer visits with his Jamaican grandmother, and the service was second to none. Miss Mabel and her niece differed on one major point—patience. The aunt had it in spades. Camilla, not so much.

A sigh left Camilla's plum-painted lips. Her nostrils flared as she smoothed the material of a white, sleeveless dress over her legs. Her gaze wandered around his office while she inhaled a deep breath and squared her shoulders.

Shaz got the feeling she was searching inside herself for some level of calm. He hoped she found some because the interruptions were part of his routine. Everybody's situation was urgent. Not just hers.

"One moment, please." He picked up the handset and slid a glance at the display. Elise, his assistant, was on the intercom.

"Shaz, I have a call about a Khalil Germaine. The person on the line insists on speaking with you. He says it's urgent. A letter also came from him just a few moments ago. D'you want me to bring it in?"

"No, I'll get it when I'm leaving." His brows contracted, and he sat up straight. Why was someone on the line other than Khalil? Did something happen? What was the letter about? Did it have anything to do with the package he had received a month ago?

The back of his neck tightened, and he resisted the inclination to rub away the tension. Other than that mysterious communication, Shaz hadn't heard from Khalil in ages, so despite Camilla's problem, she had to wait. "You can put the call through, Elise."

He could swear smoke floated from Camilla's ears as he opened the line. "Shaz Bostwick," he said, ignoring the delicate fingers tapping on the arm of her chair. "Did something happen to Khalil?"

"He's in the hospital and needs to see you." The man's voice was well-modulated but tinged with worry. "He sent a package to you a month ago. Did you get it?"

"My assistant has it." While his heart beat in loud, painful thuds, he asked, "Which hospital?"

"Northwestern."

His equilibrium returned along with his manners. "Thank you. By the way, who are you?"

"I'm his son, Vikkas."

A flash of memory brought the image of a young high school friend with olive skin, intense dark eyes, jet black hair—the very image of Khalil himself. Shaz was about to end the call when it occurred to him that he still didn't have a handle on the situation. "Hey, what happened to Khalil?"

"He's been shot."

He gripped the arm of his chair and squeezed hard as his chest tightened. "So how—"

"We're waiting on a surgeon that specializes in the delicate operation he needs to arrive. My father specifically requested that you see him today. As soon as possible."

The air whooshed from Shaz's lungs, and he pushed back his chair as the man on the line bade him goodbye.

Khalil couldn't have been hurt too badly if he was making demands such as this. But still ... it had to be urgent if he'd stipulated that he visit today.

Shaz got to his feet and picked up a black key fob. Then his gaze fell on Camilla, who he'd forgotten was with him. "I'm sorry. I have to go."

Her eyes widened, then her face fell. "But—"

"Let's reschedule for tomorrow." He closed her file, then walked around the desk, intending to show her out.

She rose and stood in his path, tipping her head a little to meet his eyes. Her powdery, yet musky perfume surrounded him in a fragrant tide. The smooth reddish-brown skin, reminiscent of clay, was several shades deeper than his. He tucked a hand in his pocket to stem the urge to touch her.

A line formed between her eyes. "What time tomorrow?"

Shaz ran a hand over his locs and shuffled his feet. "Speak to my assistant. She'll organize it."

"This is important," she said, her tone insistent.

His hand went to his neck and he blew out a gust of air. "I know, and I'm sorry. Something urgent has come up and—"

"With all due respect." She raised a manicured hand. "I was here first." After a pause, and a lift of her chin, she added. "My business is important too."

Her voice had the quality of a radio announcer's, pleasant and melodious. Unlike Cassandra, the woman he'd been seeing months ago, whose voice was so rich she practically purred when she talked. Shaz pulled his mind off that track and tuned back into Camilla.

"I agree, but I really do have to go." He wanted to remind her that he had bent over backward to accommodate her aunt by squeezing her into his already full schedule. She didn't have the right to make demands. When he looked into her eyes, he swore they went liquid. Her disappointment hit him in the stomach like a physical blow. Camilla's jaw trembled, then she sank her teeth into her lip. Then she stepped back and stood straighter. She stared at his chin as if she couldn't bear to look directly at him. "I'll speak to your assistant."

She turned away, and he followed, conscious of the way she carried herself. Her fighting spirit could fool the average person into thinking she was okay. But the anxiety that hung around her told Shaz she wasn't.

Camilla was in a situation that would make most people crumble in defeat. Not this woman. Her regal bearing gave the impression of someone much older, with a wealth of experience. Something about her reminded him of his mother, who'd gone through more than most women he knew. God knew she was still going through flashes of hell with his brother, Martin.

From what he understood, Camilla came to Chicago with her baby to access treatment for a condition Shaz couldn't pronounce. She was almost at the point where she had to return to Jamaica or be deported. Aunt Mabel had shared the story with him and appealed to him for help. Everybody in Evanston knew Bostwick Consultants was the go-to outfit for these kinds of issues, so here they were. Except, he felt like a chump because he couldn't help. At least, not now. For some inexplicable reason, he felt the need to reassure her.

He pulled in another lungful of her scent, hastened his steps, and gripped her upper arm. Camilla's skin was smooth to the touch and cool under his fingers.

Her muscles flexed, she turned and backed away from him at the same time, as if he made her nervous.

After clearing his throat, he tipped his head toward the lobby. "Don't worry. Elise will take care of everything." He gave her a warm smile. "Tell Miss Mabel hello for me."

Camilla's eyes widened, then her face softened. "She did say to tell you howdy."

Shaz reached around her and opened the door. He waited for her to go ahead of him, then pulled it shut behind them. As he went past Elise's desk, he took the envelope she held out to him. "I'll be back in ... " He changed his mind mid-sentence as he glanced at the phone in his hand, which lit up with a message. "You'll see me when you see me."

CHAPTER 5

GRANT KHAMBREL

Do what we say, and we won't dismantle your world.

"Unbelievable," Grant said, followed by a string of obscenities. He tossed back a glass of bourbon, barely tasting the smooth gold substance but instantly feeling its bite. Grant settled in his chair and pitched the letter that delivered the threat onto his desk—a beautiful 79-inch walnut and granite work of art. A gift given to him by another satisfied customer.

Grant, who, according to *Chicago* magazine, was described as a tall, fine piece of fabulously handsome architect and owner of one of the country's premier commercial construction companies, had a reputation for being an honorable and fair businessman. A clear contradiction to the allegations being leveled against him. "This is ridiculous." He reached for his glass since it was time for a refill.

"It certainly is," a familiar baritone voice agreed, as Meeks Montgomery entered the office. "You're lucky we hadn't made it home yet."

Grant placed the glass down and came from around his desk, offering his hand. "Nice to see you too, Meeks." The two men shook hands and Grant couldn't help but notice his disgruntled friend—who was his same height and athletic build only with golden-brown skin instead of Grant's olive complexion—was dressed in full kick-ass gear; a black monogrammed T-shirt, cargo pants, work boots, with a Glock 22 on his hip. He looked like he'd either just prevented a battle or ended one.

"Don't mind him," Francine Blake Montgomery stated in a matter-of-fact tone as she entered the room wearing the same black outfit and gun as Meeks. She was beautiful, petite, and a black belt who could take down a man twice her size with little effort. Francine placed her cell in the clip at her waist and stood next to her husband. "We're happy to help."

The husband and wife duo were partners in a thirty-year-old, multi-billion-dollar international security firm.

"Francine, don't you look lovely as always," Grant complimented, cutting his eyes to Meeks. "I'd hug you but—"

"He wants to keep his hands," Meeks interjected, standing with his legs slightly apart and his arms folded across a massive chest.

Francine shook her head and gave Meeks the evil eye. "How's your uncle?" she asked, adjusting her gun before taking a seat in one of the leather chairs facing Grant's desk.

Grant felt a sharp pain in his chest. His uncle, Benjamin Khambrel, Ben as he preferred to be called, raised Grant after his parents were killed in a car crash. Now the man was battling an aggressive form of cancer. "He's doing about as well as can be expected. Thanks for asking."

"Now that the niceties are over, do you want to tell me why you've brought us here at such a God-awful time of night?" Meeks asked, his irritation at being called back into the office clear.

Grant grabbed his glass, moved to the corner next to his desk, and stood in front of the bar. "Care for a drink?" He added a few cubes of ice in another glass before pouring his favorite spirit, the Pappy Van Winkle Family Reserve. This, too, was a favorite of his uncle. They often shared a libation at the end of a long week where they discussed their wins and losses. Today was a definite loss.

"Only if it's the good stuff."

"No, thank you. I'm fine." Francine crossed her legs. "I'm not drinking these days."

Grant could hear the excitement and love in his friend's voice. He walked over to Meeks and handed him the shot of Reserve. Turning his attention to Francine, he asked, "Is it safe to assume the triplets are getting a new sibling?"

"Or two," she replied, almost giggling.

"Congratulations to you both." Grant raised his glass in salute. He was sure no one would ever need to do the same for him. There would be no wife or offspring for him. After what he'd been through in life, he'd make sure of it.

"Thanks," they said in unison, smiling lovingly at each other.

"Sweetheart, now that you've finished, do you think we can find out why we're here?" Meeks ran the back of his hand down his wife's cheek, and Francine held her husband's gaze. Grant almost envied the obvious love they shared.

"Fine." She turned her attention back to Grant as Meeks dropped his hand. "What can we do for you?"

Grant returned to his desk. "This is why I called you here tonight." He handed Francine the letter as he reclaimed his seat.

"What is this about?" Meeks asked, frowning as he slid into the space next to his wife.

"The Chicago Project," Francine murmured as she read.

"What?" Meeks asked.

"He's being blackmailed," she announced.

"What the hell … you're being what?" Meeks' expression hardened as he turned his attention to Grant.

"So it seems," Grant finished off his drink and placed the glass on the desk. "Whoever's behind this is claiming I failed to disclose a previous relationship with the principals of the project, which automatically disqualifies me for the award. However, if I give them what they want—"

"Which is what?" Meeks' gaze held firm.

"I have no idea. As you can see," Grant pointed to the letter Francine passed to Meeks. "They'll be in touch."

"Where's the envelope?" he asked, accepting the note from his wife.

"My assistant has it in a file somewhere. It was delivered by messenger," Grant explained.

"We're going to need it," Francine stated, silencing her ringing phone after checking the screen.

Meeks read the note.

Congratulations on your big win. Too bad it won't last. Since you failed to disclose your previous relationship with an owner, your bid is disqualified. We can help you with that. Do what we say, and we won't dismantle your world. Keep things business as usual, Mr. Khambrel. We'll be in touch.

"And the note was attached to the award letter?" Francine questioned.

"Yep." Grant frowned and said, "Their way of reminding me how much I have to lose," he explained, running a hand across his cheek, the five o'clock shadow reminding him it was time for a shave.

"I'm guessing you *didn't* forget to disclose any past connections with the owner," Francine concluded.

"No, we didn't forget," Grant confirmed, reaching for another folder that sat on his desk and handing it to Francine. "I checked each set of proposals before they left the building."

Francine flipped through the pages in the folder. "Sounds like an inside job."

"Yeah, we just need to know who's inside," Meeks added, scowling.

"Most of my senior staff have been with me for years, and for the last two years, your company has been responsible for vetting all new hires," Grant reminded Meeks.

"That's what I mean. The breakdown could have come from either side. Remember, we provided you with the estimated cost for the project's security."

Francine raised her eyes from the documents and leveled them on Grant. "There are three projects listed. Exactly how much net revenue did the Wirtz business generate?"

Grant sat up in his chair. He felt like he was in the witness box of a courtroom. "Ballpark ... fifty million dollars."

"Damn, man, you didn't think to bring us to the table?" Meeks complained.

Francine rolled her eyes and raised the folder in her hand. "You're telling me that you made fifty million dollars from three mid-level projects over the last three years from the same company that has now awarded you with a *five hundred-million-dollar* contract?" She gestured to the pages on his desk. "Even with the disclosure document, this seems excessive. Without it, things look shady as hell for both you and Wirtz. If I didn't know any better, I'd think you were a crook too."

Not exactly the words Grant wanted to hear.

CHAPTER 6

MARIANO "RENO" DELUCA

The phone and cup of scorching hot coffee flew from Reno's grasp as he entered the brightly lit building and was met with a violent shove in the back. He did his best not to have a face-to-face meeting with the marble floor as he landed on his knees and braced a hard fall with the palms of his hands.

"Boss, are you okay?" Skyler Pierson asked, scurrying from the front desk in an effort to come to Reno's aid.

The police sirens drowned out his response. Lately, the sounds were a regular occurrence on the corner of Seventy-Ninth and Cottage Grove, a once-thriving area that had been a coveted spot to settle in its heyday.

"I am so sorry," a woman with a thick African accent said as she glanced around, clutching a small duffel bag. "Is this the Second Chance at Life Women's Shelter?"

"Yes," Reno replied, getting to his feet and wiping the knees of his slacks. He made eye contact, and the woman glanced away, but not before her woeful russet brown eyes penetrated his soul.

Slowly stepping backward, the woman said, "This does not look like any shelter I have ever seen. Where are the beds and people?"

The lobby resembled a hotel setting with soft music playing in the background, a front desk, sitting area, modern paintings, and recessed lighting. Off to the side was a cubicle for privacy, where clients provided information for the type of shelter they were seeking. Once approved, the women had access to the highly secured upstairs living quarters where the kitchen, beds, and showers existed. Safety and privacy were the top priorities.

"They're safe, as they should be," he replied as Skyler rushed to the mini kitchen and brought back some paper towels. "How may I help you?"

"I was told to ask for Mariano DeLuca. Are you him?"

"Yes."

"I am Zuri Okusanya," she whispered, then damn near jumped into his arms at the loud voices of men swearing as they walked past the entrance.

A sweet, berry-like fragrance infused his nostrils as Zuri's thick hair swept across his face.

She obviously wasn't from the community; or the surrounding neighborhoods, for that matter. Or maybe Reno had become desensitized to the everyday happenings in the Chatham community he once called home as a young boy.

"You don't have anything to worry about," Reno reassured. "That's normal." *Unfortunately.*

"My father may have sent them…" Zuri said with a trembling voice, rushing past Reno and hiding behind the front desk where his assistant, Skyler, was now stationed again.

Reno rushed over just as Skyler squatted and placed her hands over Zuri's.

"Miss," Skyler said softly. "You're safe. No men are allowed in here, except Mr. DeLuca. We have an all-female staff, down to the cleaning crew."

"I won't let anyone hurt you. I promise," Reno said, extending a hand, hoping Zuri would trust him enough to grab hold.

So many of the women who sought shelter from an abusive spouse or boyfriend were left feeling leery of all men. He had come under fire for his stance on staff gender, but the well-being of the clients came first.

"You can trust Mr. DeLuca," Skyler soothed, her manicured hand stroking the woman's trembling one. "He helps women every day who need a safe place to stay."

Zuri's eyes pooled with unshed tears, then he felt the heat of her gaze on him as he swept out the front door and had a heated exchange with the men who were creating all of the chaos. He returned as if nothing out of the ordinary had happened.

Reno's cell vibrated, but he ignored the call, thinking it was family. His parents hosted a mandatory monthly gathering to spend time with their children since everyone's business ventures kept them occupied. He was running behind. At that pivotal moment, Zuri's needs took precedence. Establishing trust with a woman entering the shelter for the first time was vital and had to be handled with the delicacy of a precious flower.

"He helped me when I had nowhere else to turn," Skyler admitted, squeezing Zuri's hand. "It took me two years to get back on my feet after my husband moved his mistress into our home. He put me and our child out while I was pregnant with our second, leaving us homeless and without money."

Zuri's glance shifted to Reno.

"We'll take good care of you," he vowed, returning her gaze, entranced by her beauty.

Reno's phone rang a second time, then a third. He ignored those calls too.

Zuri placed her focus back on Skyler.

She nodded and whispered, "We got you."

"All right," Zuri murmured, releasing a sigh. She placed a hand in Reno's and gradually rose.

The touch of her velvety skin was enough to send a shock of something he couldn't name coursing through his veins. He'd never felt so connected to a client before. This wasn't healthy, nor was it right, and he made a mental note to spend as little time with Zuri as possible.

Once she stood to her full height, Reno released her hand, then helped Skyler to her feet.

He examined Zuri's heart-shaped face. Though worry was etched in her expression, he witnessed the tension ease a little. Her lips weren't as taut, and the rosy color in her cheeks blended more with her natural skin tone.

Reno parted his lips. "Let's get—"

This time, the office phone rang.

Neither he nor Skyler could ignore that phone. It could be a woman in need or another shelter seeking information about a vacancy, of which they only had one at the moment.

"I'll do the intake," he said to Skyler, escorting Zuri to the cubicle with two crescent swivel chairs, a desk, and an iMac.

Before they could get started, Reno's attention immediately zoned in on the fast-approaching clicking sound against the floor.

Skyler knocked on the partition and rushed in. "You have an important call."

"Take a message. I'll call them—"

"The man said to tell you it's Kaleb Valentine."

Conflicted, Reno slowly moved forward. Kaleb only called the shelter if he couldn't reach him on his cell. Even then, only in cases of emergency.

"I'll finish," Skyler insisted. "Go on. We'll be okay."

Zuri nodded and gave him a wan smile.

"Thanks," he said, then turned to Zuri. "I'll be right back."

Jogging to the desk, he lifted the phone and pressed the flashing red button. "Hey KV. What's up?"

"Khalil was shot and—"

"Slow down, Kaleb." Reno pulled the receiver away from his ear. He couldn't have heard him right. Bringing the phone back to his ear he asked, "What did you say?"

"Listen to me, man. Khalil. Was. Shot."

Reno's hand flew to his forehead. "Shot—not killed—meaning he's still with us, right? When did this ...? Where? By who?"

"I tried reaching you—several times," Kaleb said. "I'll head out to Chicago and meet up with you to get you up to speed."

"Don't bother," Reno countered, glancing at his watch. "I'm on my way to the hospital now. See you soon——"

"Hold up," Kaleb blurted, getting Reno's attention before he ended the call. "Vikkas said for you to meet him at The Castle."

"All right." Reno slammed the phone down, ran to the back office, and grabbed his car keys. He dipped his head in the cubicle where the ladies were in a hushed conversation. "I'll be back as soon as I can."

Zuri stood, visibly shaken. "How are you going to protect me if you're not here? Didn't you say only women are in this place?" She lifted her bag from the floor and holstered it on her shoulder. "I better go."

Reno stepped inside, shoving the keys into his pocket. "Please don't leave," he begged, taking her hands in his. "Someone close to me has been shot. I have to get to him." He waited a few moments for that to absorb. "Whatever you're seeking refuge from, we can help you. Promise me you'll stay here with Skyler until I get back."

They gazed into each other's eyes for what felt like an eternity but was closer to a few seconds. Reno couldn't break the connection if he tried. Zuri had pulled him in without any effort and that disturbed him on so many levels. Many women of all ethnic backgrounds walked through the doors of the center. None of them had this effect on him.

"Reno, you need to go," Skyler reminded him, clearing her throat.

"Not until I get an answer."

Zuri was the first to break eye contact, releasing Reno of the hold she locked on him. Pulling her hands away, she responded, "I'll stay."

Something about Zuri Okusanya made Reno feel like she could be "the one". The timing was certainly unfortunate. What was he going to do? He could never get involved with a client.

"Great." He smiled and high-tailed it out the door.

CHAPTER 7

VIKKAS GERMAINE

"Go get your wife," Khalil Germaine whispered, his voice barely sounding above the hum of the machines monitoring his vitals in a private room at Northwestern Hospital. The wait for the specialist to arrive seemed an eternity.

"Dad, I haven't agreed to marry that woman," Vikkas replied, giving his father's hand a gentle squeeze. "Though Mama thinks I don't know she's already conspired with Damini Gupta's mother. They're so sure I'll say yes, that they've already made it well past the initial preparations."

"Go get your wife," he insisted, then crooked a finger to bring Vikkas closer. "That smart, pretty brown-skinned girl."

Vikkas flinched and stood, straightening to his full height. Just the thought of the one who pushed him away all those years ago evoked pain and sadness. "Milan?"

"Yes."

"You know the family expects me to marry Damini. Why bring Milan into it?"

"*They* expect you," he countered, and his voice was stronger than it had ever been. "I never did. While they have me in surgery, go find her."

Go find her. Vikkas drew in a sharp breath as his heart missed a beat.

He perched on the edge of the bed, being careful not to sit too close and cause his father any pain. Though that might not be a factor since the intricate traction system they had him hooked up to, and the pain meds should have meant he was as comfortable as they could make him. "It can wait. I want to be here when you wake up from surgery."

"Then I won't wake up until you arrive," he replied, and a small smile lifted the corners of his mouth. "And I want news of her."

A slight tremor of anticipation centered into his soul at the thought of reconnecting with the girl who once stole his heart, then crushed it with one sentence. When the bullet grazed Vikkas last night, and the others hit Khalil, her image flashed through his mind. The only regret he had in life. He hadn't seen hide nor hair of her in over fifteen years. He'd never find her in the small time his father had allotted.

"My planner is in that hidden compartment in my briefcase in that small closet," Khalil said. "She works at a community center—"

Vikkas stood, bracing himself on the silver railing. "You kept tabs on her all this time?"

"The bigger question is … *you didn't?*"

He held in his answer, settling on one of the leather chairs positioned near the window facing a view of lush greenery and tree-lined hills. He could tell his father was having a laugh at his expense. "That was another life. She abandoned our dreams."

"Did you ever ask why?"

Vikkas didn't have the heart to give his father an answer, but his silence said it all.

"No?" Khalil inhaled and let it out slowly. "So, you let that sting of rejection keep you from finding out the truth."

We can't do this, Vikkas. I won't come between you and the people you love.

Her words replayed in his head like a song on repeat.

"She said she'd already lost her mother; she didn't want me to lose mine."

"Did her mother transition?"

"No," Vikkas said, feeling chastised.

"Then what did she mean?"

Stung, Vikkas sidestepped the question with a major observation. "She could be married, have children, and a whole life by now."

"Are my other sons on the way?"

Other sons. Men who were love-related, not blood-related. "Yes, they'll be here when you get out of surgery. All except Dwayne, who they wouldn't pull out of class."

"I'm not going into surgery until I speak with them."

"Dad, you can't keep delaying this."

"I'm not moving," he said, eyes locking on the contraption they'd put him in once they realized the placement of the bullets required a world-renowned specialist to ensure he didn't become a quadriplegic. "The bullets aren't moving, either. It'll keep. I *will* talk with them before my eyes close."

"No talk of dying."

"Who said anything about dying?" Khalil shot back. "There's this thing called anesthesia and all that."

Vikkas tried not to laugh but failed. "You're killing me, Dad."

"Find Milan, my son," he whispered. "And open your heart ... again."

CHAPTER 8

DRO REYES

"It's about time it got here," a young man griped, scanning the untidy apartment littered with bottles and signs of leftovers from days past. "I'm starving."

"Then, don't you think it's time you answered the door?" his friend pointed out.

"Oh, right. Hang on," he yelled across the room. "Be there in a sec."

He halted halfway there. "Give me some money."

His friend shook his head. "Uh-uh. I covered the drinks. You take care of the food."

Another bang echoed through the room a second later.

"Okay, okay."

When he made it to the door, he glanced through the peephole and squinted. Unable to see anything but brown, he yanked the door open.

"Here, hold this."

He grabbed the bag. "Why do I—"

"Ow!" He fell to the floor, the contents of bag holding takeout Chinese food littering the marble-tiled entryway. Grabbing his nose, he glared up at Dro. "What the heck did you do that for?"

Dro backtracked to close the door before yanking the man up by the collar. He dragged him along behind him.

"Whoa, what the heck are you doing, man?" his friend demanded as Dro practically flung the other man onto his lap.

Dro growled, "Where are they?"

"Who?" Rolling his bleeding friend off him, he stood. "I don't know—"

"You don't want to play this game with me. I'm giving you one last chance. I suggest you shut up and think about your next answer."

"Do what he says," his friend murmured, still cupping his damaged nose.

"Where. Are. They?" Dro repeated slowly.

Glaring back, the man stood defiant for a few moments before he gave in. "The bedroom."

Dro ran down a hall on the other side of the suite. When he returned to where the other two men were, two frightened young ladies were on each arm. One was a barely concious Nina Cherry. A knock on the door prompted him to action. He opened it to find a tall, muscular man standing on the other side. He passed both women into his care.

"Take them to the car, Joe. Make sure no one sees you."

His bodyguard of eight years nodded, hoisted one woman over each shoulder, and disappeared down the hall.

Dro closed the door and faced the two men.

"Look, we know those girls," the more talkative one began.

"Oh?" Dro crossed his arms over his chest. "What are their last names?"

The ringleader's ivory face turned crimson.

"Smile."

Dro whipped out his cell phone and snapped their pictures. He included the drugs and alcohol strewn on the coffee table.

"Who are you?"

"Listen, Derrick."

The boy frowned and shrank back. "How do you know my name?"

"I know much more than your name," Dro countered. "I know where you live, work, play, what you ate for breakfast, and the hideaways you like to frequent."

Flipping through his pictures, Dro shoved his phone under their noses. Both men looked away.

"Did you touch them?"

They didn't pretend not to understand what Dro meant.

"What if we did?"

Dro laid a punch into his stomach.

He doubled over in pain. The air rushed out of his mouth in a loud whoosh. "No," he coughed out. "No, we didn't."

"Trust me; you're going to want to be straight with me."

"We are," they said in unison.

Dro unzipped his jacket and retrieved an envelope. He opened the folded papers and placed them on the table. Taking out a pen, he slammed it down. "Sign these. They're NDA's. I presume you know what these are."

"I work for a trading firm. I think I know what a non-disclosure agreement is," the leader snapped.

"That's good, Derrick. Lucky for you none of your posts thus far included my client's daughter—"

"Wait, how'd you—"

"If I see anything on social media or hear about a word either of you has spoken about this night, we'll have to have another discussion," Dro continued. "It won't be as pleasant."

Dro didn't wait to see them agree. They scribbled their names before he snatched up the documents and left them to contemplate the error of their ways.

* * *

The sun was up by the time Dro maneuvered the black Audi R8 Spyder into a carriage style garage at the back of his house. He strode across his fenced terrace and into the back door. He was passing through the kitchen when Travers sauntered in from the walk-in pantry.

"Ah, welcome home, sir," he said in that clipped British accent. "Would you care for some breakfast?"

"I'll pass, Travers. I need a shower and a few hours of sleep."

"I'll see that you're not disturbed," Travers replied.

He slid up the back stairway to the second floor. Walking down a small hallway, he took the next flight up to his private wing. After showering, Dro collapsed into bed, grateful for his blackout shades. He had just about drifted off when his phone vibrated. For a second, he contemplated not answering.

"Reyes here."

"Hi, Dro, it's Lola. Did I wake you?"

Lola Samuels was the most gorgeous nightmare he'd ever met. She was a public relations guru who never took no for an answer. She worked for Alistair Mayhew, a land baron from one of Chicago's first families, and notorious for shady business dealings. That alone was reason enough not to deal with her.

"Would you hang up if I said yes?"

"Not a chance."

Dro sat up and leaned his back against his headboard. He took a moment to clear his head. "So, what do you want?"

"I want you."

Dro's eyebrows shot upwards. "I'm sure you do."

Lola didn't miss a beat. "Don't flatter yourself. You know this is strictly business."

"Well, that's too bad."

"Focus, Reyes," she continued. "Mr. Mayhew's son is in trouble. I need your help."

He knew Shawn well; just another privileged rich boy who had too many toys and not enough ambition.

"Lola, even if I were interested in helping you, which I'm not, it certainly wouldn't be for Shawn Mayhew."

"You're the best in the game, Dro. Everyone knows it. Help me with this, and you can write your own ticket."

"I can write my own ticket without helping Mayhew," he shot back.

"Adiós, Miss Samuels."

"Dro, wait—"

Smiling, he disconnected the call mid-sentence. It was no secret that he loved trading barbs with Lola. Each of them gave as good as they got. She must be desperate, indeed, if she reached out to him to help with one of his family's sworn enemies. She was smart with a sharp wit, had a luscious body, and an infectious smile, but he still wasn't taking the bait.

Travers tapped on the door twice but didn't wait before he entered.

Dro glanced toward the doorway, surprised at his actions.

"There's been a development, sir," he said quickly.

"Can it wait, Travers? I'd like to catch a few more winks before I jump into the fray," he teased.

"I'm afraid it can't. Mr. Germaine is in the hospital, Sir. He's been shot."

CHAPTER 9

*G*RANT *K*HAMBREL

Grant nodded slowly, trying to keep his anger in check as two sets of eyes bored into him. Meeks and Francine were his business associates, but more importantly, they were his friends, and there were things he couldn't share.

"I don't give a damn how it looks," he snapped. Everything was done on the up and up and our bid …" He used an index finger to make a circle in the air to remind them that they were in this together. "We provided the best price to renovate and expand the United Center, which is why we won."

Meeks gave Grant a quick nod, stood, and took Francine's hand to help her out of the seat. Grant rose from his chair, feeling a bit off-balance.

"When are you leaving for Chicago?" Meeks asked.

"In about a week or so," Grant replied, shoving his hands in his pockets.

Meeks' shoulders dropped, and his jaw clenched. Grant glared at his friend. "Use your words, Meeks."

"I was headed home with plans to ravish my wife, but thanks to some asshole out there threatening both our wallets and reputations, I have work to do."

Grant pressed his lips together, trying not to let his laugh escape.

Francine gave her husband a playful punch in the side. "Don't pay him any mind. We'll start by looking into everyone who touched the proposal before it left this building. I'll send someone to pick up the envelope tomorrow." Francine turned and smiled up at her grumpy husband. "Everything will keep until morning. That ravishing thing you had in mind, that's still happening."

Meeks gave Francine a quick kiss, grabbed her hand, and pulled her towards the door. "We'll give you an update in a couple of days," Meeks called out over his shoulder as they swept out of the office.

Grant threw his head back and laughed. That was something he didn't think he'd do again any time soon. He was happy for his friends, but more importantly, he was pleased to have them on the case. He hated withholding information from them, but he couldn't share the whole story. They already knew enough. Too much, and it would put them in unnecessary danger.

Grant reached into his pocket and pulled out a crumpled half sheet of paper containing a second note he'd received.

First, you use dirty money from a gangster to start your business. Then you fail to disclose the necessary information for a government contract you're bidding on. You have access to something we want. Help us get it, and we'll help you. We'll be in touch, Mr. Khambrel.

"Damn." Grant balled up the paper and hurled it across the room.

Grant had spent years trying to make things right and keep certain deeds secret. He had no intention of stopping now. His cell vibrated, and he checked the time. It was too late to be receiving a call from a number he didn't recognize.

"Grant Khambrel."

"Mr. Khambrel, this is Katrina White, and I'm a nurse at Northwestern Memorial Hospital in Chicago."

"How can I help you?"

"I'm actually calling to advise you that there's been an incident, and Khalil Germaine has been admitted."

Grant's heart rate increased at the thought of his former mentor and teacher—someone he hadn't been in touch with for years—being injured.

"What kind of incident?"

"Mr. Germaine is in critical condition. You're listed as one of his emergency contacts. Can you come?"

Grant's knees buckled, and he perched on the edge of his desk. Khalil was as much of a second father to him as his uncle had been. He fought back his fear and found his words. "Yes, of course." He stood and grabbed a notepad from his desk. "I'll get there as soon as I can." After jotting down all the pertinent information, he disconnected the call, rounded his desk, and placed his things in his briefcase with one hand while he dialed his pilot with the other.

Once he'd made flight arrangements and then contacted his uncle's caregiver, Grant ended the call.

In less than fifteen minutes, Grant had made it to his loft on the outskirts of downtown Houston. He owned the top floor of a historic warehouse that had been converted into loft-style living spaces. He loved the open concept and the Cathedral windows with a view of the city. Usually, it was a welcome sight. Tonight, he barely noticed the lights of the city illuminating his living room.

Grant called the hospital as he made his way home to advise them that he would be arriving soon. He'd showered and changed. Besieged by concern and sadness, Grant stood in the middle of his living room, staring out the windows. The two most important people in his life were fighting for their lives, and there wasn't a damn thing he could do about it.

As he reached for the keys, his cell vibrated again.

Grant checked the screen, and the number was blocked. "Grant Khambrel."

"Mr. Khambrel, we told you we'd be in touch." The deep voice laughed. "See you in Chicago."

CHAPTER 10

VIKKAS GERMAINE

The moment Vikkas laid eyes on the bronze beauty, his heart started beating so fast he actually believed someone would question the sound.

All the memories of their time together in high school came flooding back. The long talks about the differences in East Indian Culture and survival and strength of those in Black American culture, the ways they would change the world, spirituality versus religion—all the things that showed their depth of understanding the lessons Khalil imparted. He remembered walks around the grounds of his home, making plans to have their own one day, with children who would be loved and cherished. Even then, he had sensed a sadness she never allowed him to explore.

"Can I help you?" A woman with an ebony complexion and bright purple hair more fitting for a punk-rocker, sidled up a little too close for his comfort.

"No, but she can," he said, raising his voice as he gestured to Milan, who had left a glass-encased office, rounded a set of desks and stood several feet away. People had left their desks and were crowding around to bear witness to whatever drama was about to ensue.

"What if she's not available?"

"Cut it out, Toni," Milan warned, positioning herself near the reception area and crossing her arms over an ample bosom. "What are you doing here?"

"I love you. Always have. Never stopped."

"Oh," Toni snapped. "It's like that, huh? Let me take my happy ass back to my desk and get some popcorn."

Vikkas watched the woman's slow progression before Milan laid eyes on him again.

"You still love me? So what do you want ... a medal?" Milan moved backward until she perched on the edge of Toni's desk and presented Vikkas her chin. "Do you think I spent the last fifteen years of my life waiting to hear you say those words?"

While Milan appeared to be angry, she had winced at his words and her breathing hitched the closer they came to each other.

"Of course not. I think life just gave me a wake-up call that I need to live my life for me—and not by my family's expectations."

Her lips parted as though to question him. Then she remained silent as though she was too shocked by his statement to say a word.

"I was not going to let another minute pass without coming for you." He touched her cheek, the skin as soft and supple as he remembered. "Is there some place, way deep down in your heart that has a little kernel, just a mustard seed of love that I can water and get to grow?"

"Oh, it's going to take a lot more than water," she scoffed, dark brown eyes twinkling with mischief. "Try that white picket fence, the house with shutters, acres of land and—"

"Done."

Milan flinched as though he had struck her. "I'm joking."

"I know," he said, gesturing toward what he believed was her office. "Where's that business plan that I know is stashed somewhere?"

She hesitated a moment, then maneuvered past the curious co-workers, made it to her office, and reached into a leather tote. She pulled out a small leather planner, came back to him and flipped to the back pages where a full-on financial projection, profit and loss statement, and marketing strategy been reduced to fit into one small set of pages.

Vikkas had to focus and push back thoughts of how good Milan's silky skin felt under his fingers. He scanned the contents for several moments, trying to ascertain the bottom line to make her an offer he hoped she wouldn't refuse. "Two hundred grand is all?"

"Is all?" Toni piped in, ignoring Milan's gesture for her to stay out of it. "What kind of stripper poles do you think we hit around here?"

"I'll cut you a check as a starter to get working on this," he said passing the planner back. "As my wife, I don't want you working for anyone but yourself."

Milan's head tilted; her dark brown eyes widened to the size of saucers. "Wait a minute. Who said anything about becoming your wife?"

"You didn't say anything about not loving me either," he countered. "One thing happens after the other. Basic math."

She chuckled. "Still a smart ass. You can't just come in here, sweep me off my feet with all these lofty promises and expect me to upend my entire life for you."

Vikkas angled toward a tall woman who had an air of authority about her.

"I'm DaniMari Conchita Raye Alonzo," the woman said, extending her hand, her complexion flushing with a bit of color.

"Your whoooooole name," Vikkas teased.

"Long story," she shot back. "Dani for short."

"How much notice does she need to give?" he asked, placing his hand over hers.

"Can we have a week?"

Milan's perfectly arched eyebrows shot up. "Traitor," she said to a woman he had correctly presumed was her boss, then focused on Vikkas again. She bit her bottom lip and held his gaze. "I can't believe you're doing this."

"That makes two of us." He glanced at the digital clock on the far end of Toni's desk. "I'll come back for you as soon as I resolve this family emergency."

"Come back?" Milan said, her voice laced with worry. "What happened? What emergency?"

"Getting shot can change a whole lot of perspectives," he confessed. "Someone tried to take my father's life and I was caught in the crossfire. The only thing I thought was that I spent all this time helping my father to change the dynamics of world progress and missed out on the best woman there is."

"Girl, you'd better quit playing and give him some before I drop both pairs of drawers and give him a slice of Heaven," Toni teased, placing a hand on Milan's shoulder.

She glared at Toni before Vikkas said, "She lost me at both pairs of drawers."

"Trust me," Milan said, holding up a hand to ward off any further query. "You don't want to know."

"And the only Heaven I need in my life is right here in my arms." Vikkas picked Milan up, carried her over the threshold of the exit as she struggled in his arms, did an about-face, then brought her back to reception, and set her upright.

"What was that for?" she asked, peering up at him as though he had lost his mind.

"Your favorite movie," he replied in reference to *An Officer and a Gentleman.* "You said back then, that if a man can't come for you like that, he shouldn't bother."

"You remembered," she whispered, and the tenderness of her expression felled him.

"There's a lot I won't ever forget." He gave Toni the stink-eye, hoping she'd back up a little. "Personally ..." He shifted his gaze to Milan. "I thought you'd be giving me a hard time."

"I would've if it wasn't for this," she said, sliding a folded, worn-out sheet of yellow paper from a side pocket of the planner. She handed it to him and he glanced at the hand-written words...

I intend that I am experiencing a relationship with love, compassion, respect, joy, peace, purpose, passion, contentment ...

"Intentions?" he said, scanning the rest of the list detailing the type of relationship she desired, and ones for her home, business, self-care—a range of things about a page long.

"Yes," she whispered. "I've said these words every day, without fail, for two whole years."

"So, what makes today so different?"

Milan exhaled, then put her focus on him. "Last night, I got a little angry at God that it's taken so long on the relationship end of things and I said 'If it's going to be a minute, could you send me a placeholder until the real number comes along?" She cupped his face in her hands. "Today, you walked back into my life."

"Awwwww," Toni crooned, and he could swear he saw several women wipe away tears as they whispered their own brand of appreciation.

"So, am I the placeholder or the real number?"

"Time will tell, Vikkas Germaine," she whispered, placing her hand on his. "Time will tell."

"Awwwww. Our very own *Coming to America*." Toni snapped her fingers and whipped her arm in a wide loop. "Sexual chocolate!"

"He is *not* chocolate," Milan protested, groaning her frustration.

"Okay, then." She repeated the movement, adding, "Sexual caramel."

"Doesn't have the same ring," Vikkas teased without taking his eyes off Milan. "I have to get back to the hospital."

"Hospital?"

"My father's in surgery right now."

"Then what the hell are you doing here?" Milan nearly screeched.

"Before the specialist made it in from D.C., he practically demanded I go and find that smart, pretty brown-skinned girl. He said, 'I always liked her.'"

"I liked him, too," she said, and there was a warmth emanating from her that brightened those words.

"Hey, give me a second, I'm going to call and check in on things," he said and Dani pointed toward her office.

"It'll give you some privacy."

CHAPTER 11

The moment he was out of earshot, Dani whispered to Milan, "So what's the deal with you two. Why didn't you all make a run for it back then?"

"Too much had happened. A lot of it Vikkas knew nothing about. I never wanted him to know how cruel my family had been."

* * *

"Don't you bring none of them pale folks to this house," Pearline warned. *"Got that White man after you, sniffing around like a dog in heat. All he wants is what's between your legs."*

Milan couldn't even protest that Vikkas Germaine wasn't White, because in her mother's eyes, anyone who wasn't Black was painted with the same broad stroke.

"What's he see in you?" she snarled, her voice dripping with contempt. *"Black girl from Englewood. Already got them folks gassing you up, making you think you smarter than the rest of us."* She cackled. *"Yeah, go on off to that fancy school. You'll be right back here with the common folk before too long."* She put her dark-eyed gaze out the window on a group of men huddled near the curb, handling some type of transaction that no one in the neighborhood would tell the police they*

had witnessed. "Better get you one of them dope boys, worry about schooling later."

Laughter from her siblings, aunts, and uncles made Milan bristle with embarrassment.

"Wasn't Daddy one of those dope boys?"

The laughter came to an abrupt halt.

Pearline did a swivel that nearly made her land on the tattered carpet. "So whatcha trying to say, heifer?"

"When does he get out of prison? Next ... what? Ten, fifteen years? What's him being in prison done for you?" Milan locked a steely gaze on her mother. "And you still had to make it on your own, struggling to raise all of us. Is that what you want for me?"

Pearline's eyes narrowed to slits. She crossed the distance until only a few inches existed between them. "Are you sassing me?"

"Just stating facts. Grandma said the minute a woman puts her faith solely in a man to take care of her is when she gives up every ounce of her power."

"So, you think you're the one with the power, huh?" Pearline taunted with a low throaty chuckle that sent a shiver of alarm up Milan's spine. "All that book learnin' done went to your head." She inhaled, swept a look at all of the expectant faces in the room, and smiled. "Well, Wonder Woman, lasso your little brown ass upstairs and pack your shit. How's that for power?"

Aunt Ruthie was on her wide feet in a split second. "You're taking this too far, Pearl."

"Go on, girl. Git."

Milan slid past her mother, then the sisters lounging on the sofa and floor who didn't bother to hide their sneers. She trudged up the stairs, went to the tiny bedroom she shared with three others, grabbed her birth certificate, learner's permit, social security card, and the cash hidden on the underside of the dresser that her late grandmother had given for emergency purposes. She tucked that into her bra, slid her schoolbooks into her backpack, retraced her steps while struggling not to cry. She would not let her mother see those tears. Though inside, sadness and fear had taken root. Only two more years and she would've been out of this place for good. Why couldn't she keep her mouth shut and absorb the verbal blows as well as she had the physical ones?

At the foot of the stairs, Milan found her voice. "One day, Mama, you're going to need me. When they"—she gestured toward her drug-dealing brothers—"land in jail. And these four," she said, looking at her sisters, who glared back at her. "Have a few more babies running around here." She took in a breath, and hoisted the backpack on her shoulders. "When no one can help you and you're unable to help yourself, I want you to think about the day you turned me out into the street simply to prove a point. Remember it, Mama. Because you're going to have to forgive me in advance for one reason alone. I can't say what I'll be able to do for you when you've made it your business to make my life hell."

That being said, she swept out the door with nothing more than essentials and a prayer that she would land on her feet.

* * *

"I haven't seen any of my family since that day." She focused on the guardian angel on Toni's desk, trying not to let her gaze wander to Vikkas. "That crew in high school," Milan said to Dani. "They were the best. Not because they were the most intelligent by academic standards. There was something about them. I mean, all the students there were smart. But that Khalil crew, they were focused and intense, had that extra something that made them charismatic. Without question, you knew they were going to be somebody. They were going to succeed at all costs. All of their goals in life were set early on—they didn't date around because getting a girl pregnant was not part of the plan—marriage and family when they were ready was. They . . ." She lost her train of thought the moment Vikkas' gaze locked with hers through the glass while he was still engaged in a phone call. A jolt of desire shot through her body. "Mr. Khalil put them and nine girls on a learning track that was different than everyone else."

"Then why didn't you walk down that aisle after you graduated?"

Milan would never admit it, but marrying Vikkas would have been one of her greatest joys. Honestly, it still would be.

"Mr. Khalil didn't have a problem with Vikkas being with me, but his mother certainly did." She frowned at the memories of that ugly exchange that nearly caused Vikkas and one of his uncles to come to blows. "He would've lost the rest of his family if he had married me instead of one of the Indian girls they had picked for him. I couldn't do that to him. My mother was a piece of work, but I still loved her. I …. No, I made the right choice."

"So, you gave up your happiness for his?" Dani said, her focus drifting from Vikkas to Milan. "Suppose his happiness is all wrapped up in yours?"

"Why are you so sure about us?"

"Why wouldn't I be? Early on, he was all too ready to do whatever it took to be with you. That kind of love isn't something to be dismissed. Ask me how I know." She flexed her left hand, displaying a gold wedding band. They both looked at Vikkas through the open slats of the blinds of Dani's office. "You'd better recognize and give yourselves the chance you didn't have."

Vikkas stepped out of the office, looking every bit the successful businessman in a suit that draped his athletic build to perfection. His olive complexion, dark hair that grazed the tops of his shoulders.

"Get out of here," Milan said to him when he approached. "I'll stop by the hospital after I'm done here today."

"One other thing …" He reached into his wallet and slid a credit card in her hands.

"Black card?" Toni said, gasping, along with a few others.

Low whistles and whispers of approval echoed in the office.

"I need you to pull up stakes for a minute and stay at a hotel if you're not comfortable moving into my spot for a while."

Milan glanced at the card, but his grave tone is what made her stiffen. "Vikkas, what else are you not telling me?"

CHAPTER 12

KALEB VALENTINE

A chill snaked up Kaleb's spine then a slight smile split his sienna complexion, while he pulled a red pearl Genesis G70 into the circle drive of his cousin's mansion in the heart of Gross Pointe Shores, the home resembling the castle he visited on his last trip to Chicago and what he witnessed.

"Okay, Z." Kaleb stepped out of the vehicle, speaking to no one in particular. "I see you're doing the damn thing."

The sounds of jazz and the aroma of grilled chicken rode on the gentle summer breeze as Kaleb approached the sand-colored, three-story manor that had been festively decorated with lilac and gray balloon sculptures. A framed, hand-painted sign that read "Welcome the Babies Gray, Amir and Zarina" stood to the side on a door that was flanked by cut glass sidelight windows on each side.

Kaleb pulled a cell phone from his pocket and looked at the screen, trying to forget the last call he made to his best friend, Reno.

Khalil's been shot.

His own voice echoed in his mind as images of Khalil and Vikkas haunted his thoughts.

Kaleb's heart sank thinking about Vikkas Germaine and how he had reached out to him as a request from his father, Khalil. As kind as Khalil had always been to him, Kaleb strayed away from any involvement with him and his leadership, a decision that brought about an avalanche of turmoil on top of his already traumatic life.

He walked into the empty foyer prepared to follow the joyous laughter when, from the top of one set of the double staircases, a bouncy, blonde preteen stopped almost mid-air in her descent.

"Who are you?" she asked, the smile she wore dropping from a face the color of milk and honey before she backed up the stairs the way she came.

Kaleb flashed a warm smile at the girl, trying to hide his confusion for being questioned by someone who was not only a child; but also a stranger to him. Extending two large golden gift bags, he stated, "I'm Kaleb. And you are, young miss?"

The youngster tilted her head and narrowed a pair of bright hazel eyes, possibly noting Kaleb's taller-than-average height, athletic build, freshly trimmed beard, and the tattoos that peeked over the top of his black long-sleeved t-shirt.

"I'm looking for my cousin, Zephyr Gray."

With deliberate hesitation, the girl completed her descent, keeping an eye on Kaleb before running in the direction of the noise that echoed from the living room.

Moments later, Zephyr appeared in crisp, creased blue jeans and a white t-shirt, locs pulled back, while holding a slick-haired baby on his shoulder.

"Wassup, Special K?" Zephyr greeted Kaleb with a hug as he balanced his wide-eyed daughter.

"Not as much as you, cuz," Kaleb retorted with a chuckle. "A man gets left alone for a minute to expand his empire, and you decide to get a whole wife and family."

"You know I'm always on the move," Zephyr said with an answering chuckle of his own. "When you know something is right, why wait?"

"And you're not looking any worse for wear." Kaleb adjusted his gifts so he could stroke the baby's hair. "I can't even hang with any of my boys because they're talking and looking like old men after one child."

"That's because they aren't doing it right," Zephyr said with a hearty laugh. "I see you met Nadira."

"Something like that," Kaleb replied, following Zephyr toward the living area. "She just kept staring at me like she was trying to read my soul."

"Nadira is a little intense," Zephyr admitted, describing his young sister-in-law.

Kaleb stretched his neck to examine the entryway dominated by an oversized crystal chandelier. "Not too shabby," he said, impressed by the three-story foyer.

Zephyr practically beamed. "It's cozy, I'll give you that."

"You call a nine-thousand-square-foot house that backs up to the Detroit River 'cozy'?" Kaleb gave a low, throaty chuckle. "Okay."

"Come on. Mom and Dad are waiting to see you."

Zephyr led the way through the busy main floor of the house that had been eclectically decorated with large, colorful floor pillows, tall greenery, and African and Persian art displayed on every wall.

Instrumental melodies of familiar R&B songs played while Kaleb followed close in step behind his cousin as they walked upon a two-tiered deck that spanned the length of the back of the estate. A buzz of conversation rose from below them. Men, women, and children milled about on the lower level, distracting Kaleb for a few seconds.

Zephyr took an opportunity to honor his wife with a kiss before peeking under a blanket covering his nursing son. His mother, Helen, hopped up from her seat on the patio.

"Kaleb, come give your auntie a hug." Bright yellow chiffon floated as the woman opened her slender, but shapely arms wide to receive the young man she helped raise after unfortunate and deadly circumstances caused him to leave his home in Chicago.

"Hey, Auntie." A boyish grin spread over Kaleb's face as he lifted the woman off her feet with his embrace. "I see you're working out," Kaleb said, gently squeezing her bicep with his thumb and index finger.

"I'm trying to keep up with Angela Bassett." Helen snickered at her reference to the gorgeous actress.

"Hey, Unc," Kaleb yelled across the deck to Zephyr's father, who was flipping chicken breast and turkey kielbasas on the grill. The salt-and-pepper haired man gave a brief nod.

"K, I want you to meet my wife, Aisha," Zephyr said, drawing Kaleb's attention away from his mother to place it on a Persian beauty with reddish-brown hair and brilliant green eyes.

Kaleb turned to Aisha, who had adjusted her clothes under the blanket, and lifted the covers from a curly red-haired little boy.

"Nice to meet you," Kaleb greeted, extending a hand toward the woman who kept her attention on the baby in her arms.

Aisha stood, cradling her son. "It's good to meet you, Kaleb," she said with a warm smile. Turning to Zephyr, her eyes sparkling at the man who close family members knew had changed her once horrific story into something beautiful, she chimed, "I need to change and feed Zarina, Babe. Wanna trade?"

"It's my turn with my grandson," Helen teased, crossing Zephyr's reach to receive the baby. "Always trying to keep my grandbabies from me."

With a kiss, Zephyr handed the baby to Aisha, and she disappeared into the house.

"Your wife is lovely, Z, but what's with the women in your house leaving me hanging when I try to shake their hands?" Kaleb inquired, placing the gift bags down near the chair Aisha had vacated.

"When I tell you it's a long story, K, it's a *long* story," Zephyr explained with absolute ambiguity.

Kaleb's eyebrows shot up to his hairline.

"So, we have a little business to discuss," Zephyr said, quickly changing the subject as they strolled to a private area of the backyard.

"Indeed."

They each took a seat on a wooden bench at the farmhouse table behind the bustling preparation activity on the deck.

"First, let me thank you again for your investments in my projects here in Detroit."

"First," Zephyr's gaze intensified on his cousin. "Let's talk about what's good with you. How is Special K handling life right now? Award-winning real estate developer and soon-to-be-married man."

Kaleb's eyebrows drew into the middle of his forehead as his face twisted as if he smelled something rank. "Soon-to-be married? I don't know what anyone has told you, but Meme and I broke up over a year ago. Keep up, man."

Zephyr's eye grew large with the news.

"Let's just say there was a disagreement with her business practices, and it almost cost me the company and some jail time," Kaleb explained, pulling out his phone and tapping the screen. "I've kept things quiet while I processed the situation. However, this beauty right here..." Turning the device to Zephyr, the dark orbs of a copper-skinned woman covered the screen. "Skyler Pierson."

"That name sounds familiar," Zephyr said. "Didn't I hear you mention her in a conversation about some business with Reno?"

"Yeah," Kaleb said, the corners of his mouth lifting as he shoved the phone back in his pants pocket. "But enough about me. The business at hand ..."

"The business at hand," Zephyr repeated, beaming at his cousin.

"You've had an excellent return on our current investments, right?"

"The property on Jefferson still needs to be occupied. Other than that, I can say the return has been decent." His gaze narrowed to slits. "Get to your point, K."

Kaleb laughed at his cousin's impatience. Zephyr was never one for dancing around a subject.

"I'm looking into a few properties in the Chi," Kaleb stated while Zephyr flexed his long, tapered fingers before lacing them to settle on the table. "I'm already in line to work with Common on his vision for the renovations of the Avalon Regal Theater in South Shore. And there are a few properties that I think will be good for us to acquire before property values go up and they're out of our reach. I've made a down payment on a small, three-door storefront complex on Stony Island and I paid cash for a house I want to renovate. The area is established but needs some fresh development. What do you think? Are you in?"

Zephyr sucked in a deep breath, glancing over Kaleb's shoulder at Aisha, who sauntered onto the deck with the baby.

"Did I miss something?" Zephyr's tone held a ring of concern. "There's a reason why you're not in Chicago now and haven't been there for the last fifteen years."

"I know, but this is a great opportunity," Kaleb expressed, trying to ease an unspoken worry.

"That's too close," Zephyr warned, lowering his tone. "You may have walked away from that life, but I'm sure there's at least one member of your crew who remembers what you did before you left. A six-foot-four, two hundred sixty-five pound, curly-haired dude is gonna be hard to miss whether you're wearing Ralph Lauren or jeans and a tee—or not."

Kaleb leveled a steely gaze on Zephyr's hardened expression. "Most of my set is dead or in jail. And all of that 'other life' happened before my mom sent me to live with you," he declared. "I don't think I have anything to worry about."

"K, what about the whole reason you had to come here in the first place?" Zephyr shifted on the bench. "It wouldn't be hard for a surviving family member to find you. So I have something to worry about even if you don't," Zephyr explained. "You know I'm always down for a good investment, but what I'm not going to do is help you write your death certificate … or mine." Zephyr nodded in the direction of Aisha and Nadira holding the twins. "Do you see the parts of my heart that now live outside of my body? I won't take one step that could jeopardize their safety. I'm not even sorry to tell you this."

Heat rose up Kaleb's neck as he listened to Zephyr deny his request. The breeze from the river was the only thing keeping him cool at the current moment. Kaleb felt a vibration from his pocket. Grabbing his phone, he recognized the Chicago area code on the screen, but the rest of the numbers weren't familiar.

"Valentine speaking."

"This is Officer Washington of the Chicago Police Department. Your name was given to us as the owner of a home on West 89th."

"What's the problem, Officer?"

"The property in question is the focus of an arson investigation," the officer clarified.

"Arson?" Kaleb's elevated tone caused a few guests to turn in his direction. Zephyr's eyes widened at the one-sided news.

"We need to have you come into the precinct to answer some questions about the property."

Kaleb ended the call, giving Zephyr a wary glance.

CHAPTER 13

Jai swept a gaze across the nine men who were situated around the boardroom table. Their expressions matched exactly what the moment called for—solemnity. In his heart of hearts, he still couldn't believe that one of the men he trusted would do something so … monstrous to one of their patients. Not them. Not when they had been given a second chance at life.

Chetan afforded them and so many others a chance to get into a field that had been off-limits because of their past mistakes. Jai had taken a gamble, even when the industry had come out publicly against his actions. The fact that his patients were healing and recovering at a staggering rate only proved Jai's methods were sound. But it did not keep medical heavy-hitters from taking swipes at him during symposiums, in industry journals, and in the news. Success was its own brand of karma—good and bad.

Now it looked as though his detractors would have even more reason to attack him, this place, and his choice of employees. Each one of them sitting at the table, wearing bright blue uniforms and specially fitted sneakers, were well-groomed with everything from locs, braids, bald heads, and fades. No one could look at them and tell the hard life they'd had before walking through the doors of a place that had been Jai's dream.

"Let me tell you what's about to go down," he said, landing a hard gaze on the men one by one. "The police were notified. The first thing they'll do is question each and every one of you. I have several lawyers on the way to represent you, and they'll have access to money to bail you out if it comes to that. Do not speak to the police without your lawyer." Jai settled his thoughts, trying to think of every possibility so they wouldn't be caught off guard. "Then, they'll want a DNA swab. It should be no problem to clear yourself that way. Make sure to do it under the direction of your counsel."

"Now you know they can change those things in a minute," Hiram, the most vocal of the group, said. "That woman in Alabama owned a lab and messed up those drug and DNA tests—on purpose." He shared a glance with his coworkers. "If they want one of us for the crime, they'll find a way."

Jai thought that over for a minute. The young man who had created some of the artwork on the center's walls had a right to be concerned. Investigators were still trying to determine how many parents lost jobs and custody of their children because of what Brandy Murrah had done.

"You're right," Jai conceded. "I'll have Kelly bring in an independent lab to do our own testing. Maybe two, if it comes to that and if their results come back a little strange. That way, we'll have something to work with in proving they altered the results."

"That's straight, man," Michael said, slumping his lanky frame down into the leather chair.

Falcon nodded, giving a toothy grin. "Thanks."

"But how are you repping us like this and you don't know who did it?" Kevin asked. A tense silence fell over the room.

"Most of you have been with me from day one," Jai replied, leaning on the edge of the table. "There's no way in hell you'd jeopardize your career by letting your dick do something that will destroy your life and everyone else's."

Mumbles of assent echoed from the men. A few nods and affirmative statements followed.

"Besides, if I'm wrong, then only one of you should be under fire. I'm not going to let the rest of you pay that price."

"That's what's up," Hiram said, scanning the ones closest to him. "This whole thing feels like someone is setting you up—us too."

Jai rounded the table until he was standing behind an empty executive chair. "I hadn't thought of that. It's definitely something to consider. I can't believe that my instincts were that far off."

"You got us lawyers," Chuck stated, but his expression was far from happy. "So, we get bailed out and then what do we do? I didn't take any kind of vacation until y'all forced me to since they don't roll over to next year."

"That's because everyone should take a break," Jai protested, once again glad he had instituted that policy. Getting the men to take time off had been an uphill battle—something he had not anticipated.

"But where am I gonna go?" he shot back.

Hiram nodded. "Our people are going to be all up in our grill about this. You *know* the police are going to blow this up. It'll hit social media. We're not gonna be able to leave the house or anything like that without some reporter all up in our face."

"And you know once people find out we're ex-cons," Mike added with a pointed look at Jai. "We're gonna be guilty without being given the benefit of anybody's doubt."

A sudden pall of sadness fell over the room, and it was almost tangible. That, too, was his biggest fear—these men, who had worked so hard to pull their lives together, would be tried in the court of public opinion. None of the things they'd done since leaving prison would be taken into account.

"And you know how it goes," Hiram said. "The police are gonna find a way to pin it on us. They *want* us to be guilty."

"Not going to happen on my watch," Jai shot back, but he understood that the wheels of Chicago justice often became stuck and mired in all kinds of underhanded political dealings. "As soon as the police process you or do whatever it is they're going to do, I want you all to go home, give your folks a heads up, get a good night's sleep, then come to this place. Every day." He held up a card, then gestured toward the notepads and pens stacked up near the teleconference phone in the center of the table. They each grabbed one, and he rattled off the address for them to jot down.

"You won't be allowed back into the center until this all blows over. So, you'll meet me here."

"And do what?" Hiram said, frowning at what he had written on the paper. "Sit around and look at their ugly mugs?"

A few chuckles released the tension in the room.

"No, you're going to be here every day, nine-to-five like you're coming to work, and you're still going to receive a paycheck."

Falcon's gray eyes widened to the size of saucers as he said, "Word?"

"Word."

All the men perked up and Jai made eye contact with them. "We're going to filter through every document, every video, everything we can get our hands on."

"Why?"

"If we can't trust law enforcement to do their jobs, we're going to do it for them," he answered. "Between all of us, we'll figure out who violated Temple Devaughn. The police don't have their lives or livelihood hanging in the balance. We do."

"What do you mean *we* White man?" Hiram joked.

Jai smiled at the reference to the Lone Ranger and Tonto from an old television series. The crime-fighting pair once found themselves surrounded by hostile Indians. The Lone Ranger asked Tonto, who was an Indian, "What are *we* going to do, Tonto?" To which Tonto replied, "What do you mean *we*, White man?" The Lone Ranger was the one most likely in trouble because of his pale skin, and the Indians were less likely to take out one of their own.

Jai hated to point out that in the challenge they now faced, he and the male employees of the center were all underdogs. The enemies coming their way wouldn't differentiate between him or them.

"First of all, I'm not White, I'm East Indian," he corrected. "What I mean by '*we*' is—you, me, and everyone who is caught up in this."

"But this isn't going to hit you as hard as it hits us," Hiram said, swiveling in the chair.

"Chetan is my center—*our* center. I have my nuts in a sling just like you do."

"Facts, fellas," Falcon said, tapping the edge of his notepad. "Let's get this done."

Hiram stood, moved to the head of the boardroom table. "You all know enough that together we can figure this out." He was silent a moment. "Someone violated our patient. We should be pissed because they did it on *our* turf and *our* watch. And they did it to someone who trusted us to protect her."

Kevin gave a head nod. "Word."

Jai glanced at his watch. "I'll have Kelly bring copies of the same things that the police are given—visitor logs, employee swipes, video. We, and I mean the nurses and doctors, too, missed something seven months ago. We won't miss it now."

"Wait a minute," Hiram said, getting to his feet. "I mean, when the child is born, DNA will tell them all they need to know."

"By the time that happens, all the patients will be moved, the place will be virtually shut down. There won't be a center or a job to come back to."

That admission from Jai was met with a lengthy silence.

"You are well aware that those who are proponents of traditional medicine and Big Pharma have been after this place from day one. And I'm about to expand, too?" He shook his head. "That will give them a swift kick in the rubber parts. Our methods and holistic practices have proven far more effective than modern medicine. That's not good for Big Pharma and for the industry. The fact that we have an eighty percent success rate is hitting hard and making people question all the ways that doctors are feeding into the system and pumping patients full of one drug after another, causing them to need more drugs, and masking the issues instead of pinpointing the cause."

"Jai, all of them have arrived," Kelly said, sliding halfway into the room and tapping her watch. "You have to go. Now."

"Fellas, your lawyers are here," he said walking to the door. "I'll be in touch."

CHAPTER 14

"Something's about to go down. I want you protected," Vikkas confessed to Milan.

"Does it have something to do with that bandage that you've been trying to hide since you walked through the door?"

He grimaced and adjusted his arm. "I didn't want you to be concerned, but my father has called in all of his sons to set his house in order. There are some people who don't care for the fact that they're about to be displaced."

"Will you be safe?"

"We will, from this point forward. Daron and Calvin, a security specialist and an inventor, both have the technology to keep everyone on point. Including you."

Her expression turned somber, and he checked his watch, gauging that he had about two hours to get back north. "On second thought, I need a handwritten note from you. My father is not going to believe I found you."

"So, you're in the habit of lying?"

"Not at all, but this was so important he delayed his surgery to tell me to get my wife."

"He meant me?"

Vikkas nodded. "Damn straight."

"I always liked that man."

"Seems like the feeling is mutual." He gestured to her planner. "Where's that picture of your dream house?"

"How do you even know that I would ..."

"Some things never change," he countered, causing Toni to sigh loudly. "You were always a visual person. You'd keep that image in your mind until you have it."

Milan navigated to her photos and handed him her phone this time.

"Oh, it went from a house to a condo?"

Then he whipped out his phone and swiped across a set of images. "Will this do?"

"Dayuuuuuuuuuum," Toni crooned as everyone crowded around, peering over Milan's shoulder.

"Near the water?" Milan asked.

"Wilmette. Right on the lake."

She swiped a finger across her screen and made the image of her dream place disappear.

"No," he said, placing a hand over hers. "We can still have that spot. We'll need a place in the city."

"My God, does he have a brother for this sister right here?" Toni said, ignoring Milan's warning glare.

"Let my father tell the story, I have several," Vikkas confessed.

Toni scratched her head at that admission, but there was also a salacious grin that signaled she would eat a man alive with all that lusciousness.

Milan placed a hand over his, saying, "I want to believe that this can work. But there was so much working against us." She then explained what happened the day she and her mother were at odds.

"Do not let your mother's words take root in your soul," he warned, placing a hand over hers. "Not a single one. You hear me?"

She nodded, and he pulled her into the wall of his chest.

"Maybe I wasn't strong enough to see what was going on," he said. "And maybe we wouldn't have made it at such a young age. So life might've had the right idea even if we didn't understand it." He lifted her hand to his lips, placed a gentle kiss on the fingertips. "But we're grown-ass people now, and family doesn't get to have a say."

"I am not going to turn into a blubbering idiot," she said, her voice wavering.

"Girl, gon' and cry," Toni encouraged with a dramatic flourish of her fleshy hand. "And give that man some ass while you're at it. I'd like to watch."

He turned his focus to the director. "Where do you get these freaky employees?"

Dani gave him a sheepish smile and a shrug along with a comedic lift of her eyebrows.

Vikkas playfully slapped a palm on his forehead. "Oh Lord, not you too." He steered Milan away from Toni and her boss. "I'm getting you out of here before they corrupt you."

"Too late," Milan confessed. "And I want to come to the hospital with you," she said, tucking her tablet and planner in the leather tote and glancing over her shoulder at Dani. "I'll be back, but I need to do this."

"Actually, let's gather up some of your things and let me get you settled in first," Vikkas said with a glance at his watch.

"Go. Go," Dani said, shooing both of them toward the exit. "We're not going anywhere."

"Take good care of our girl," Toni yelled after them. "She's got a tribe that'll put up bail money."

"I'll keep that in mind."

"And we want an invite to the wedding," Dani said.

CHAPTER 15

Kaleb placed his cell on the wooden table and braced himself, his mind filtering through what the officer had said.

"What happened?" Zephyr questioned.

"The house I told you about is now the focus of an arson investigation. Chicago's not-quite-finest want me to come in for a chat." Kaleb's mouth went dry as he gave the report.

Zephyr shook his head and wiped a hand over his face. "Wow … that escalated quickly."

Rubbing his temple, Kaleb watched other guests smiling at their children running the yard. He wasn't sure if he should mention the tragoc events of his last visit to Chicago, or that he had been in the vicinity of where a crime had been committed at all. Before last night, he hadn't seen Khalil or Vikkas since his hurried exit from Macro Prep and the subsequent middle-of-the-night exodus from his hometown.

"Z, man, I guess we have enough business to handle for now," Kaleb declared, not fully expressing his real concern for returning to his birthplace.

Thoughts of Reno swirled in Kaleb's mind, the only friend he had managed to stay in touch with since leaving Chicago, a friend who was never a part of his gang life and had never judged him. Kaleb was supposed to forsake everyone who wasn't affiliated with The Sovereign

Kings, even siblings if they didn't want to join, but Mariano DeLuca was the secret he kept. If not for the death of Kaleb's father to a rival set, they would've started living their dream of building up South Chicago way before now. To Kaleb, now was as good a time as any.

"K, you good?" Zephyr asked, rocking Amir whose young aunt dropped off the fussy infant.

Kaleb offered a slight smile as he took a turn to hold the chubby-cheeked baby. "I get it, Z," he relented, memories of his own father flashing through his mind. "I have to get on the road. Duty calls."

"Where?"

"Back in Chicago. I have to have a sit down with the detective."

"You know what? Just take my jet again," Zephyr offered. "I don't want you in Chicago any longer than you have to be."

Kaleb took a moment to absorb the beauty of his cousin's generosity, and he pushed back on the memory of the previous visit and the questions that darkened the optimism of future plans. "First, I don't set foot in the Windy City for nearly fifteen years. Now I've hit the place twice in two days. What are the odds of that?"

Zephyr shook his head. "Cousin, you're courting trouble." He clapped a hand over Kaleb's shoulder. "C'mon, Special K. At least stay long enough to get a plate or two," Zephyr suggested. "We need someone with a huge appetite to help us eat all of this food."

Zephyr and Kaleb laughed, but Kaleb couldn't shake the worry his cousin had thrown out there. He wasn't wrong. Possibly, one member from the rival set who might still be looking for him.

That fire might have more implications than the CPD could know.

CHAPTER 16

"Excuse me, Nurse …" Grant read her name tag. "Mary. Isn't there anything you can tell me about Khalil Germaine's condition? He's my father."

"Your father," she repeated, her left eyebrow raised, skepticism front and center.

"Yes, I'm his son, and I need to know his condition." Grant's voice raised an octave, then he heaved a sigh. "My apologies, I'm just worried about my father."

"I understand. Let me see what I can find out." She stood. "Excuse me for a moment."

"Thank you." Grant turned and leaned against the nurses' station. He glanced up and his gaze collided with the greenest eyes this side of the Chicago River.

They were on the face of the most beautiful woman he'd ever had the pleasure to observe. She was about a foot shorter than him, physically fit, and the pantsuit she wore showcased her curves. When she smiled, showing off a perfect set of white teeth, his heart did a few cartwheels. Her hair was pulled back in a tight bun, and Grant's hands itched to run through what he could only guess were the kind of dark silky strands a man could get lost in. Her demeanor and outfit screamed sophistication.

Grant was worried about his mentor, but there was something about the stunning woman mere feet away from where he stood had captured his attention. Before he could close the distance between them, he heard, "Mr. Khambrel …"

He smiled and nodded at the gorgeous stranger before turning his attention back to Nurse Mary at a desk that housed several women in brightly colored uniforms. "Yes."

"This way, please."

Grant glanced over his shoulder in time to see his mystery woman being led out of the reception area by an older man. "Of course, but what can you tell me about my father's condition?" He followed her down the hall, where signs indicated they were headed toward the ICU. They stopped in front of a set of double doors. "*Please…*"

"All I can tell you is when Mr. Germaine arrived, he was in critical condition. They stabilized him, but the specialist hasn't made it into Chicago." She swiped her badge across a scanner, and the doors opened. "Follow me."

Grant felt as if he'd been hit in the chest. He flexed his whole body to stay upright.

"Mr. Khambrel, are you coming?" He looked up to see Nurse Mary was already through the door, standing, waiting for him.

"Yes." Grant quickly made it to her side, and she led him to a waiting room down from the ICU.

"You can wait here. The doctor will come to find you when it's time."

"Thank you," he said as he watched Nurse Mary leave the room.

Grant stood in the middle of the empty room, fighting his fears. He took a seat in one of the low chairs, allowing his mind to flashback to the beautiful stranger he never got to meet.

CHAPTER 17

The brightly lit path dimmed as Kaleb continued down the hospital hallway toward the voices of men—some that were vaguely familiar to him.

"Who could've done this?" one voice whispered.

"I need some answers," another voice quietly demanded.

Kaleb arrived to see a small group of well-dressed men who he had crossed paths with on occasion while hanging with Reno when at Macro along with two investigating officers who looked like they'd had a few donuts too many. All of their expressions reading somewhere between stress, wariness, and anger.

"Can we help you?" one man asked, breaking away from the small group that was congregated in the waiting area.

Grant. That's his name.

"I'm Kaleb. Vikkas asked me to meet him here."

Each of the men glanced at each other, before leveling a gaze on Kaleb as though to inform him that his presence wasn't desired or appreciated.

"I know who you are," Grant said, glaring at him. "Your reputation precedes you."

Kaleb narrowed his gaze on the man. "My ... reputation? As an award-winning real estate developer? You know, for building Detroit deserts into metropolises. Is that what you mean?"

Grant moved in closer, nostrils flaring as though he was keeping his temper at bay. "I don't know about all that, but I do remember you from Macro and who you ran with outside of school. You could be the reason that—"

Kaleb's eyebrows drew in, his lips twisted in confusion at the crux of the unfinished accusation.

"And then you disappeared." The man who he remembered as Daron stepped in. "Now you're here. What are we supposed to think?"

Kaleb never wore a gang jacket to school—affiliations of those kind were strictly forbidden at Macro. But as a kid who was not fully initiated, he wore a great deal of black and gold—colors of Sovereign Kings.

"We've been trying to get in touch with Reno all morning because Khalil—" Daron expressed through clenched teeth.

"Why did Vikkas ask you to meet him here?" Grant inquired, holding up a hand and effectively shutting down any information that was about to be shared.

Kaleb could feel his face harden from the unexpected and unnecessary interrogation. "I'd rather not say."

"Listen," Daron said, taking the edge off of his tone. "I'm sorry we're reconnecting under these circumstances, but now we're in a holding pattern. If you have any information about what happened to Khalil we'd like to know."

CHAPTER 18

Kaleb would love to confess what he saw at The Castle before coming to the hospital, but Vikkas had advised against it and swore him to secrecy surrounding the crime. He would not break the man's trust.

"All I know is Khalil was shot," Grant snapped, closing in on Kaleb's space.

"I know," Kaleb said, stepping out of the area he unwillingly shared with his rival and resisting the urge to push him out of his face.

"How do you know?" Daron asked, his tone dropping several pitches as he shot a fixed glare on Kaleb. "That's a better question."

"I'd rather not say," Kaleb responded, standing by the exit door to the private waiting room, hoping Vikkas would make it there soon and put an end to this verbal sparring that seemed to come from a place of pain. He'd give them a little allowance given the circumstances, but when this issue with Khalil's health was concluded Kaleb was going to deal with these men on his terms.

"That seems to be your response for everything," Daron spat, crossing the distance and approaching Kaleb.

Kaleb balled his fist at his side prepared to make contact if necessary.

"Where the hell is Reno?" Grant asked Kaleb, giving him a once-over that sent a ripple of anger up his spine. "Didn't you used to hang with him all the time? Why isn't he here?"

"We've been trying to get in touch with him all morning," Daron remarked, placing a steadying hand on Grant's shoulder. "No answer."

"I'll get Reno here," Kaleb assured. "I have other business to tend to, gentlemen. I'll make sure he gets in touch with one of you."

Kaleb reached for his phone. Retracing his steps back to the hallway, he dialed Reno's cell, and it went straight to voicemail. He ended the call and called the safe house Reno owned in hopes that he would answer. More than likely, he was working with a client.

"Thank you for calling The Second Chance at Life Women's Shelter," a warm voice answered. "You're speaking with Skyler Pierson. How may we support you?"

"Hey, Skyler. It's Kaleb," he answered, a sense of urgency coloring his tone.

"What can I do for you, Mr. Valentine?" Skyler inquired, a note of tension in her voice.

"I need to speak with Reno."

"What's your concern?" Skyler asked, as if she had never met Kaleb before this call.

Kaleb released a weary sigh, realizing that Reno's gatekeeper was going to block any avenue to his friend at the moment.

"Tell Reno that Kaleb called and I'm at the hospital right now. Some of our old classmates are waiting for him to get here. I have some police business to handle and might not be here when he arrives."

"Wait one second," she said. "I'll go get him."

Kaleb held on a few moments, grateful that Skyler relented. He couldn't stop thinking about the one man who recognized him and held such animosity, his fury as tangible as if it were under his skin. The prevailing question is where his anger came from?

"Hey, where are you?"

"Had something come up," Reno answered. "Instituted an emergency protocol and moved all of the women in the shelter to a safer location. Right now the police are all over the place because three men landed on the business end of some semi-automatics and the morgue." He took a deep breath. "Where are you?"

"I'm back in Chicago. My flight arrived early. I received a text from Vikkas to come to Northwestern Hospital because Khalil needed to speak with me," Kaleb explained, regretting that he left Khalil even at Vikkas's request. "Even in Khalil's condition, the man is still trying to conduct business. A couple of fellas are here waiting for you to show up," Kaleb said, turning his back to the men who were watching his every move. "It was pretty intense. One dude said he recognized me from Macro and remembered who I used to run with. He all but accused me of having something to do with what happened to Khalil."

"Man, you've got to be kidding me," Reno replied, sounding as exasperated as Kaleb felt. "Which ones—"

"It doesn't matter, but I'm angry that they would even accuse me of harming Khalil. I mean, I'm not as close to him as you are, but still."

"Khalil was a mentor to all of us." Reno paused, and Kaleb could practically hear the man's thoughts churning. "He'd never condone how they treated you."

"It's all good," Kaleb assured Reno with a nervous chuckle. "I've been treated worse."

"It's not all right," Reno countered. "At any rate, I'm on my way to The Castle."

"I'm headed to the precinct."

"No, stay there until I arrive. I need to set some things straight when it comes to you."

"All right. I'll be here when you get here," Kaleb said, ending the call.

He put his focus on the men in the waiting room, who were now looking at him with undisguised suspicion.

"I guess I'll be here until Reno gets here," he informed the men as he covered the distance between them. "But I need to make better use of my time. I have phone calls to make."

CHAPTER 19

Four hours later, Reno drove through the wooded grounds that led to acres of sprawling greenery and onto The Castle property in Wilmette. As many times as he'd seen the place, the lavish estate still filled Reno with awe. The eighteen-hole golf course, the horse stables, the tennis courts, and his favorite—the lake where he and Khalil fished during the summer—were all places of solace. Great memories were rooted there.

Vikkas had texted to say Reno should meet him at The Castle because the police called and wanted to speak with Vikkas about some details of the shooting, but he also wanted a private talk with Reno away from the others. Finally reaching a parking lot that nearly spanned the length of The Castle, Reno frowned at the overwhelming Wilmette Police presence at the typically serene manor. He hopped out of his steel-gray Porsche and rushed toward an entrance covered with yellow caution tape.

"Sir. Who are you?" a man in a dark-colored uniform asked, stepping in front of Reno with one hand stuck out to halt any further movements and the other hovering over his service weapon.

"Mariano DeLuca," he responded, halting in his tracks with a steady focus on the officer's defensive stance and shooting hand.

"What business do you have here?"

"Where's Vikkas Germaine?" Reno asked, side-stepping the officer to get a peek inside.

"Young man, don't make me—"

"Reno, thank God you're here," a man in a navy suit and shades said, as he came from behind the yellow tape with two officers in tow. He bypassed the officer who had kept Reno from entering and pulled him into an embrace.

"Vikkas, I'm so glad to see you," Reno said, recognizing Khalil's son, even though years had passed since they'd laid eyes on each other. "Can you tell me what's going on? Is Khalil all right?"

"Before he answers any of your questions, I need to know why the victim was asking for you," the officer inquired, easing his hand away from the gun and pulling out a notepad and pen before squinting at some unreadable portion of his notes.

"I gave you that information already," Vikkas countered.

The man's head snapped up. "In Mr. DeLuca's own words, please."

Reno glanced at Vikkas, and he nodded.

"I received a call—"

"About?"

Reno's jaw clenched at the officer's snappy tone.

"From?" The officer nudged, seeming miffed at Reno's silence.

"Kaleb Valentine."

"From … Detroit?" the officer remarked, flipping through the notepad.

"Yes," Reno replied, aggravated by the line of questioning.

"So, why are you here?" the officer asked, placing his pointed focus on Vikkas.

"I'm Khalil's son and his attorney. I don't need permission to be on the estate because I reside here. One of the detectives said they needed access to the upper rooms." He gestured to the police milling about. "Don't you all share information with each other?"

A plain-clothes female officer who was standing off to the side said, "Be sure to stick around."

"You know where I live, and you know where I'll be," Vikkas shot back. "C'mon Reno. Let's get you to the hospital."

They turned to make their way toward the parking lot, and Vikkas said, "Hold up. I left something upstairs."

Vikkas asked the officer who'd been standing guard at the entrance if he could go inside to retrieve his wallet. The officer signaled for another policeman to escort him. A burly officer blocked his entry as Reno tried to follow them, but not before Reno saw the dark stains. Yellow markers with numbers surrounded the splattered blotches.

Who would want to hurt Khalil? He was the most gentle, compassionate and—

Reno shuddered, glancing upward at The Castle's stone tower.

Khalil had been Reno's high school mentor who doubled as a stand-in when work prevented his father from being present. Their bond had grown stronger during the first years after he'd graduated from Macro, but Reno had drifted when the demands of the architectural firm he worked for became insurmountable. Then even further once he founded the Second Chance at Life Women's Shelter. Reno often referred to him as Papa K when they weren't handling business. Now the life of the man whom he loved and respected was in jeopardy.

A tap on the shoulder drew Reno from his thoughts. "Let's make tracks," Vikkas said, sauntering in the direction of the parking lot. "I want to run something by you."

"I'll drive," Reno said, retrieving the keys from his pocket.

Vikkas slid into the passenger's seat and buckled in. "Northwestern Memorial."

Reno drove in silence with nothing but the sound of the wind whizzing by to compete with his thoughts. He tried to maintain a positive attitude, but the worst-case scenarios kept creeping in. What if they lost Khalil and he hadn't so much as called the man in all these years?

"Hey, man, what did you want to talk to me about?" Reno asked, trying to refocus his sad thoughts.

"So, what's your connection to Kaleb Valentine?"

Reno frowned. "Why are you asking me this?"

"The guys are having a hard time believing that my dad included Kaleb in his plans for all of you. He was an outsider, but apparently, my father saw something worthy in him," Vikkas replied. "You're the only one who vibed with Kaleb, but we discussed—"

"Who's we?"

"Calm down, man," Vikkas countered, scrolling through messages on his phone. "My father and I discussed some things. You know, he's getting older, and he wanted to appoint you guys heads of the estate while he was in his right frame of mind. And that includes Kaleb."

"As it should," Reno shot back, still miffed that folks wanted to give his boy so much grief. "Kaleb isn't who y'all think he is, and I'm offended by the insinuation." Reno flipped on the turn signal and glanced in the side mirror before switching lanes. "I can't believe Papa K wouldn't have mentioned it to me first, before he sent you to come for us."

"He tried, but not a single one of you answered the call to action. So, I sent it personally in an envelope that outlined everything." Vikkas slid the phone in his suit pocket. "Don't get in your feelings, Reno. This is business, and it's about service to others. None of the other guys know anything about the depths of how bad things are. Don't make me regret confiding in you."

"Man, look," Reno snapped. "I don't even want to discuss this anymore. I want to lay my eyes on Khalil first. Then when he's able, he can say what he wants in his own words."

CHAPTER 20

Situated in the front seat of his vehicle, Shaz tore open the envelope and read the two lines requesting his presence at Northwestern Hospital. He stashed it in the glove compartment and said a quick prayer before switching on the engine. He'd been raised in Evanston, and though he'd traveled extensively, he chose to come back home and launch his business, thanks partly to Khalil, who encouraged him to give back to his community. His immediate family still lived in Evanston, among a strong contingent of Jamaicans. That, and the fact that he'd found friends when he first came to the States was the reason his father had chosen to settle there instead of Chicago, where his mother's relatives had migrated.

Before easing out of the parking space, Shaz took a bite of the roast beef sandwich he'd snagged from the coffee bar on the corner. As he drove, focusing his eyes on the busy roadway, the worry he'd been keeping at bay settled in his stomach and nearly killed the rest of his appetite.

He didn't know how serious Khalil's injury was, but it might be critical if he was demanding to see him right now. And what about his Macro classmates? Had they been summoned too?

Only when he arrived downtown did Shaz realize he'd been absorbed in thoughts of the time spent at the Macro International Magnet School.

He'd been part of a group of rabble-rousers, intent on having a good time while learning. Until they came under Khalil's influence. Out of the four of them, he'd been closest to Alejandro, or Dro as they eventually started calling him.

Not thinking twice about it, Shaz dialed his number and engaged the Alfa Romeo Stelvio's hands-free system. "Hey, Dro, did you get a call today about Khalil?"

"I'm on my way to the hospital right now."

"Is he—" Shaz stared through the windscreen, preparing himself for the worst.

"I haven't heard anything more. "

"I'll be there shortly."

Shaz pulled into the secure parking facility, wrapped his sandwich, and chased it with a mouthful of orange juice. When he stood outside the Stelvio, he rotated his shoulders and turned his face up to the warmth of the sun. His mother insisted that sitting in an air-conditioned office all day meant he didn't get enough Vitamin D.

He grinned, realizing Paula Bostwick would be delighted to know she was getting inside his head, as she did with all her children.

Again, Camilla and her issues came to mind, but Shaz suppressed those thoughts. The seriousness of the hospital visit set in and his smile vanished when he crossed the sidewalk and entered the brightly lit building. Cool air and the scent of disinfectant greeted him as he walked the industrial white tiles and spoke to an Asian nurse at the intake desk. She directed him to the private wing several floors up.

The elevator ride deposited him on more colorful tiles leading to a reception area with an upscale décor and a warm, welcoming feel. An exquisitely made-up nurse, whose nameplate read, Pat Walker, fielded his questions and directed him to a door on her right.

He wondered how long he'd have to wait for news on Khalil's condition.

"Mr. Bostwick," the nurse added. "A doctor is with Khalil right now, and since you aren't a relative, you'll have to wait for clearance."

"Even though my name was on a shortlist of visitors?"

"I'm sorry. Daron Kincaid set security protocols. Now everyone has to be vetted first. Even his son."

Two men were already in the room and looked up when he entered. A smile spread across his face as he recognized Jai and Grant, whom he hadn't seen in years. Both stood and extended a hand toward him. Shaz was in the middle of a handshake with Jai when the door opened again. On the threshold stood a bald, middle-aged doctor, wearing blue scrubs and wire-rimmed glasses.

"Gentlemen, Mr. Germaine isn't out of danger, but against doctor's orders, he insists on seeing you. You'll only be allowed to go in one at a time. We'll do it according to last names." He glanced at a yellow sticky note attached to the clipboard he carried. "Is Mr. Valentine here?"

Kaleb nodded and felt the heat of everyone's gaze. "That's me."

The doctor's lips tightened and disapproval shone from his eyes as though he, too, believed Kaleb was responsible for putting Khalil in the hospital. Or maybe his distaste had to do with something else because all of them received the same look.

The medic motioned to him, then turned toward the door. "Please come with me."

CHAPTER 21

After a quick visit to The Castle, which was now crawling with cops, Daron took an envelope from Vikkas and promised to swing back by the hospital after Vikkas had the opportunity to speak with the others. Daron had researched every aspect of the documents and found information that compelled him to work on changing the program he ran out of a Morgan Park facility.

Daron studied the nut-brown face of the man sitting in one of two gray chairs in front of a charred wood desk. A psychologist and educational specialist, Pedro Garcia, was key in helping young men under Daron's wing transform their lives.

Pedro looked up from a printout of the new slate of ideas and said, "You're making the program public?"

"With the reporters sniffing around and this Castle business, it's what the program requires to survive and thrive."

Daron was determined to assist these talented young men in getting off the streets and better utilizing their skills. Now that he'd given Katara decoy tracker, he expected that media attention would die down.

"You're really planning to buy land out here to build a facility?" Pedro went back to reading the latest draft of Daron's brainstorming ideas to expand and protect the program.

Daron's company being thrown into the spotlight, along with his obligations to The Castle, made him realize that another person needed to be the face of the organization he'd created to run the program. The first step in protecting the participants was building a location outside the house which was currently their meeting place. Daron clicked the screen to bring up the plans on his laptop.

Pedro straightened his stack of papers then sat them to the side. "You're risking your life to help these boys?"

"The target was already on my back," Daron countered, as he crossed another name off his list on a yellow legal pad. "And I want them to know there's something more than a street corner or a hustle that'll land them in prison."

"I get all that, but it doesn't mean you need to light that target up so brightly that even a blind man could see it." Pedro stared at Daron for a moment, like he had taken leave of his senses.

"Maybe I should pull Javier off the Florida job."

Javier was Daron's go-to person for unique architecture and construction, but he was currently working on building the estate house on Daron's private island off the coast of Florida.

"You need that place finished if anything goes sideways."

"A couple of architects who're also being considered for members of The Castle could handle the project." Daron knew making the right alliances was important, especially since at least two of the young men in the program were somehow connected to current members of The Castle.

Even though he was making adjustments, being an active managing member of The Castle was still up for debate. As persuasive as Vikkas' proposal was, Daron would be risking his freedom, a committed relationship with Cameron, and the success of his young men by accepting the responsibility.

"You also know, there are several members who'll be quite upset that you're taking the best assets off their teams."

Major truth behind that observation. Daron's opportunity for membership had placed him in the middle of a war zone and The Castle was now the battleground. The tablet resting on the table beeped loudly as his perimeter alarm went off. Pedro's head snapped up as Daron glanced at the screen. A woman swept across the lawn wearing a skintight shimmery jumpsuit and a long hair weave covering her narrow features. Despite not having a clear view of her face, Daron knew it was his over-the-top Aunt Brandi.

"I'll be back." Daron left the office and maneuvered through the entertainment room to the back door.

Due to the way the house was situated, most guests parked at the back and used the rear door. Cameron was one of the few people who used the front door because it faced Longwood Avenue, and no one could park there. A safety mechanism of her own.

Brandi extended a finger with a long glittery manicured nail to ring the bell as he opened the door.

"I heard you were back in town." She enveloped him a bear hug, then stepped back and swatted his arm. "You couldn't come to see your aunt?"

"No." Daron learned long ago not to mince words with his dad's sister. She was a master manipulator, liar, and user. He'd had experience with criminal masterminds who couldn't touch her.

Brandi swept past him and did a slow inspection of the room's fireplace and artwork before lowering herself to the black leather couch. "You always were like your father."

"You say that like it's a bad thing." Daron locked up, trying to think of a respectful but quick way to get rid of her.

"Hmph," she scoffed. "That depends on who you ask."

"Aunt Bee, what brings you here today?"

"I was seeing how you were holding up." Her voice softened as she spoke, her eyes losing some of their gleam.

Daron lowered himself onto a chair. "I'm fine."

"You don't have to pretend with me." She scooted to the edge of the couch, leaning over the arm and facing him. "While you and your brother had a difference of opinion years before his death, I know that you two had been close."

Damn. Daron forgot this was the anniversary of the day his brother,

Troy, and his family supposedly died. "It's been years. I miss them, but I have come to terms with them not being here."

Brandi sprang from the couch. "Troy was murdered, and you shouldn't let it go."

"I've had the accident investigated by a private firm," he countered. "They agreed with the police report. There's no evidence that it was anything other than a tragic accident." He wished he could ease her mind, but she couldn't know that Troy was alive and in witness protection. If certain men realized he was that close to law enforcement, they would take him out to make sure he'd never tell their secrets. Aunt Brandi couldn't be trusted to keep her mouth shut.

"They're wrong, and I won't let it go until the people who did this pay." Her hands gestured in the air, signaling a deep-seated frustration.

"Do you know something that I don't?" Daron couldn't understand why she was so persistent about this, especially after he'd made every attempt to confirm that there was nothing nefarious behind the car accident.

"You know how he earned his money?" Brandi stared at the family photos on the mantle of the fireplace. She touched the frame of the picture of Troy standing with their father. "He was just like Rook, loved the high of being in the streets."

"I thought I was like Dad."

"Troy was like your dad before he met your mother. But he gave up the streets to try to give your family a better life and I ... " She snatched her designer purse off the couch. "I'll look into it, but promise me whatever happens to me, you make sure the people who killed Troy pay." She stormed off toward the door.

Daron blocked her path. "Don't do something that'll make me have to grieve you, okay?"

Brandi might not be his favorite member of the family, but he wasn't trying to bury her either.

"I can't make any promises." She went to her tippy toes and planted a kiss on his cheek before exiting.

"Shit." Daron pulled out his cell, dialing as he watched Brandi rush to her Benz. "Steve, I need you to send someone to shadow my aunt. She's back to inquiring about Troy's accident."

"Why is it that I don't remember your aunt being that close to your brother?" Confusion seeped into Steven's voice.

"She wasn't. She benefited from Troy's ability to invoke fear and his way of lining her pockets."

Daron didn't understand why she was so convinced that Troy's death was a murder.

"Whatever the reason, I don't want her getting herself killed."

CHAPTER 22

Jai steered his Audi onto the Dan Ryan, grateful that the morning rush was over. He could make it up north without waiting in the "parking lot" that the six-lane highway normally became. The memories of the teens he'd spent a good majority of his high school years with came to mind. He wondered what he would find awaiting him, and that put him a little on edge.

Macro International Magnet School was a multi-tiered glass and stone building situated in the heart of Chicago. Teens from all over Metropolitan areas and the outlying suburbs tested into placement and were chosen by a set of criteria no one had ever been able to figure out.

Khalil Germaine, a philosophy and science teacher who had founded the school, had taken things a step further by focusing on the development of male teens from all corners of Chicago. They were taught additional subjects outside of the normal curriculum. Life skills that parents tended to mysteriously expect, but also forgot to impart to their children—balancing a checkbook, preparing for adulthood, managing crises, among other basic things like maintaining a residence and advocating for what they needed on a personal level.

He also taught them the mechanizations behind world events that were not in the textbooks all the other students had. They learned of The Birth Control Project used to control White women and the minority population. He explored the impact and true purpose behind wars that had taken place on the different continents, and the role that the United States, Britain, and Europe had played in manipulating world economies and disasters to their benefit. He also tied them to a little-known phenomenon called The Heaven Project, where a man had taken sixty impoverished women from the United States, trained them in enclaves in obscure areas of Canada, Belize, and abroad, then situated them in marriages and positions where they would wield a certain level of influence. The most powerful lesson the boys had learned was to respect women and understand that they were as important in all aspects of life as the men who were hell-bent on oppressing women and people of color on all continents.

Khalil called each of these teens *scholars*, not students, which immediately put them in a different mindset. He had given them each a mission to find their passions, but also to remember to "cover their own backyard" when they achieved a certain level of wealth and could positively impact the neighborhoods where they had lived.

Now, all of these years later, Jai wondered how the others had fared since they'd lost touch.

"Call Kelly."

The connection was immediate and so was the irritation in her voice. "Quit micromanaging, Jai. You've only been gone ten minutes."

Jai stifled a chuckle at her incredulous tone. "This is important."

"You think I don't know that?" she shot back. "I have just as much to lose as you do. This has been my life ever since I graduated from college."

True, he had hired the feisty woman whose studies in nutrition, physiology, and marketing had been an asset. Her organizational skills were nothing short of amazing. "Are the fellas still in the boardroom?"

"Yes, getting a little antsy because the lawyers have basically said be silent and let them do all the talking."

"Let me put them to work. I need you to have them look up..." He fed her the names of his former classmates as he rounded the curve under the Indiana Toll Road. "Then patch me in so they can give me the info."

"I could do that for you easily."

"I need your concentration on when the detectives show up."

"Got it. I just sent a text to Hiram, and he'll tell the others." She was silent a moment, but he could hear the swift movements on the other end, signaling she was typing out the words that would spur the men to action. "Give me a second, and I'll transfer you in there. But may I ask, who are they and what are they to you?"

"Men I think I'll run into at Northwestern. They might have been informed too."

"That's a thought."

"I'll talk to you soon."

The moment Hiram clicked in, he asked, "Do you think any of these guys had something to do with what happened to Temple?"

"No, this is about something else entirely," Jai answered.

The nine of them had followed through with good intel on his former classmates.

Grant Khambrel had made a name for himself in commercial construction. Mariano DeLuca had first amassed property in the Chatham area, then opened a women's shelter. Shastra Bostwick went into immigration law that serviced a wide range of clients who came to America from all over the globe. Victor Alejandro Reyes' background only stated that he was a businessman, but not what type of business he was in. Vikkas Germaine, Khalil's son, was making waves in international and intellectual property law. Dwayne Harper, he's currently a professor of World studies at Malcolm X College.

Jai took a glance at the envelope, frowned, and added two more names.

"Kaleb Valentine," Hiram said after a few moments. "Real estate, mostly in my old hood."

"Daron Kincaid," Falcon added, then paused. "Technology is all it says, but that's a little strange. Nothing solid on this one. He's a ghost. Both Daron and Alejandro are."

"So what's the deal with these dudes?" Hiram asked before Jai could query them further.

"I'm about to walk into something, and I want to know more about them than they know about me. Text me everything you found."

"All these dudes are rolling in dough, man," Falcon said. "How do you know them?"

"Went to high school with them," he replied, steering onto the ramp that would take him to Lake Shore Drive. "Well, eight of them."

"In Chicago?"

"Yep. Macro International."

"Ah, you mean that bougie school up north," Kevin taunted.

Mike chimed in with, "The one where all those nerdy kids hang out?"

"I don't know about being nerdy and all that," Jai defended, realizing they weren't too far off the mark.

"I can't tell," was Hiram's sarcastic reply, causing others to laugh it up and making Jai smile. The fact that they could poke fun at him with such a heavy issue hanging over their heads spoke volumes.

"Y'all doing all right?"

"Yeah, we're hanging," Hiram answered for the group. "It's a lot better because we know you've got our backs."

"Always," he admitted. "I'll see y'all in the morning."

CHAPTER 23

"I need to know Khalil Germaine's condition," Dro said to the woman at the Patient Information desk. He flickered a look at her badge and added, "He's in ICU."

Sharon looked up from her computer screen. "Sir, are you a relative?"

"Yes," Dro said without hesitation. "I'm his son."

Her penciled eyebrows almost shot up to her hairline. "Really?" A smirk inched across her red lips at his declaration. "You don't say?"

He frowned at the unexpected sarcasm. "Is there a problem?"

"Just a minute, sir."

Sharon made a call and spoke quietly into the receiver so Dro couldn't make out what was being said. She hung up and then smiled as she pointed over his shoulder.

"If you could wait there, someone will be with you shortly."

"Excuse me?"

"Please wait over there," she repeated.

Irritated, Dro was about to respond when someone said, "Family of Mr. Germaine?"

Not giving her another thought, Dro dismissed the representative at the desk and strode toward the woman waiting patiently by the glass doors.

"I'm Mr. Germaine's son, Dro Reyes."

The two women shared a speaking glance before the newcomer said, "Nice to meet you, Mr. Reyes. I'm LaTanya Wright, the hospital's family liaison. Can you follow me?"

"Thank you," he replied a little louder than necessary.

He followed her through the triage rooms and a hall lined with chairs. A few people leaned against the walls, either talking on or scrolling through messages on their cell phones.

She scanned a badge and opened a door. Stepping aside, she motioned for Dro to precede her.

When he walked through the door, he stopped short. Almost all of his former classmates from Macro were gathered in the waiting room. One had an intense focus on the cell in his hand. A few were buried in a heated discussion.

"Like I told the rest of your *brothers*," she said with a hint of skepticism in her voice, "There hasn't been a change in his status at the moment."

Dro ran his hand through his hair, standing it on end. His voice was laced with ice when he said, "The moment there's an update—"

"We'll let you know. All of you," she smiled sweetly before turning on her heels and leaving.

"You're slipping a bit, aren't you, Dro?" Shaz said, shaking his head. "Sad. I thought you'd be much older before you lost your touch with the ladies. With your El DeBarge looking self."

Chuckles echoed from Kaleb, Grant, and Jai.

Turning, Dro spotted Shaz sitting by himself. His long legs were stretched out in front of him. Dro walked over and claimed the seat next to him.

"Talk about me," Dro shot back. "You're the lawyer. Aren't you supposed to have the power of persuasion?"

Shaz chuckled. "Tried it on three different nurses. We all did. None of us got any further with Marva, Flo, Joyce, Rochelle, and Ellowyn than you did."

"Daaaaaayum," Dro taunted Shaz, the heartbreaker when they were in school. "On a first-name basis with *all five of them* and still didn't get no love."

"Maybe we should've come up with a plan before we arrived," Jai countered, waving off the men's laughter.

Reno and Vikkas stepped into the private waiting room and Vikkas introduced Reno by saying, "Not quite Cali."

"And not quite Vegas," Shaz chimed in.

"It's Reno, all the way, baby," all of the men chanted their high school taunt, then laughed and welcomed Vikkas and Reno into the circle of their embrace.

Reno's lost his smile as he pulled away and let them have it with both barrels over their treatment of Kaleb.

Duly chastised, Shaz cut in when Reno finally took a breath, and he could get a word in edgewise. "The surgeon arrived and Khalil still stalled long enough to speak to each one of us. Said he'd sent you on a mission of mercy."

"Stubborn old man." Vikkas shook his head.

Reno laughed. "Don't let him hear you call him that."

"Do they know who did it?" Shaz asked, moving until he was closer to Vikkas.

"Police are all over The Castle grounds searching for clues and collecting evidence."

"Vikkas?" Shaz gestured toward his bandage.

"Grazed my arm. I took one there when my father tried to jump in front of me while I was trying to get in front of him to protect him."

Shaz shook his head, the locs shifting with that small movement. "The man is the most peaceful person I know. We were some hardheads, but he was patient."

"Speak for yourself," Reno shot back. "*You* were a knucklehead. We knew how to act."

"See, why you bringing up old shit?"

The men shared a laugh.

Vikkas scanned the faces of everyone. "This was a professional hit, fellas. Deliberate. The only thing the shooter didn't plan on was that my father and I would change positions to protect each other. That threw his trajectory off."

"The question is, why?" Jai said, leaning against the wall. "Khalil's only been back in the country for two weeks."

"Three," Shaz corrected. "From what I've learned, he's been trying to clean up the illegal activity going on at The Castle for a while now. It's the main reason why he's back. The board wasn't moving fast enough, and most of them don't want things to change. They were hoping that Khalil would continue to stay in the background like he had been for all these years."

"His return was hardly a secret," Dro reasoned. "It was all over the news. I was working on helping him with a few issues."

"You have to admit, not one of these men who have a hand in running The Castle was happy to see him back." Shaz paused, mulling a few things over. "Khalil's arrival was the bell tolling on their shady dealings. Any one of them could've been responsible for trying to take him out."

Dro's expression turned grim. "We should've come to help out the first time he asked us to get involved. We all could've done more to turn things around before it came to this. We all have connections, Shaz."

"Not powerful enough," Grant pointed out.

Vikkas glanced at each one of them. "Did you all receive that package from him?"

"About a month ago," Shaz confirmed, and the others nodded or verbally affirmed their answers.

Vikkas fell silent. The fact that none of them had come when his father requested stung. "He needs us to unravel the mess The Castle has become. While we were traveling the world, teaching the principles of working from a higher consciousness along with racial and gender equality, the politicians he left here cut deals with crime lords and all kinds of unsavory businessmen who stormed The Castle and plundered every good thing that my father had built."

Vikkas paced in front of the group. "Now, some of the finances and properties are tied into things my father would never approve. There's even whispers that the place had been used to house women who'd been shipped from Europe in metal containers." He focused on each one of them. "It is not a one-man job. The FBI and police have their fingers on the wrong side of this pie. He needed you. I know this is a lot, and you all have your own lives—but this is bigger than us. Much bigger."

"Do you think that the contents of that envelope he sent us had anything to do with the attempt on his life?"

"Possibly. Not everyone is happy with his new moves." Vikkas paused in his movements, glaring at them. "Why didn't any of you accept his challenge?"

Silence permeated before varying excuses.

"This means whoever it is, they're trying to warn him before there's a legal change in ownership," Shaz said.

"You mean take him out," Reno said with a pointed look at Vikkas. "You would be next in line."

"Then evidently you didn't read past his Letter of Intent."

They didn't confirm or deny.

"We're not family," Grant said. "Why would—"

"If you have to ask, then you don't realize how special you are to him." Vikkas left his spot to move several steps forward into the center of the room. "He mentored boys who had more than potential. They had courage. They had strength. They had determination." His expression hardened as he asked, "Was he wrong about you? *All* of you?"

CHAPTER 24

Before Dro could respond to the question Vikkas had posed to everyone, the door opened and Marva came in with a pitcher of water and some glasses.

All the men stopped talking and rushed to the nurse's side.

"Any news?" Vikkas asked.

"Not yet," she confirmed, pouring a glass and handing it to him. "They're still in surgery."

Dro took in Vikkas' disheveled appearance and what looked to be droplets of blood on his shirt.

"Are you okay?"

Vikkas downed the entire glass as though he wished it was actually something stronger. "If it weren't for a jammed gun, I'd be dead. As it is, Dad's in there fighting for his life. I tried, but …" he said, the anguish evident in his voice. "Dad was holding his own 'til one of the intruders got the jump on him." Vikkas scanned the solemn faces in the room. All eyes were on him. "These men made it past our security and found a way into our home," he stressed. "The Castle has state-of-the-art surveillance, yet they practically walked through the front door."

"I have ears to the ground as we speak." Daron stepped forward. "If it was an inside job, I'll know about it."

"Any idea what happened to the team?" Dro asked.

"I haven't checked since Daron came through to do damage assessment and control," Vikkas replied. "Last he mentioned was that one was in critical, three others were injured."

"Did you see any of their faces?" Shaz inquired.

Vikkas shook his head. "Just one, but he didn't look familiar. He could've been for hire."

"Which only confirms this wasn't random," Kaleb observed. "The men sent after Khalil were professionals."

"You still have that woman on the media blackout?" Vikkas moved closer to Dro.

"Lola's on it," he replied. "None of this has made it to the press yet. But it'll only keep for so long. Someone on the police force might be getting paid to slide information a journalist's way."

"Snitches," Kaleb said, shaking his head. "The kind that don't get stitches."

"Mr. Germaine?"

They all turned to see a strawberry blonde woman in scrubs near the door. Vikkas moved forward. "How's my father?"

"Would you rather we go into one of the conference rooms and talk?" She gestured to an area several feet away.

"No, if there's an update, you can tell me right here. We're family," he said, motioning to everyone else. "They're my brothers."

She blinked, gave a wary glance to all of them.

"Papa was a rolling stone," Shaz taunted. "Left a few pebbles here and there."

The nurse tried to keep a straight face as everyone rushed to Vikkas' side.

"Well, your father made it through surgery, but his condition is still tenuous. We were able to retrieve the bullets and stop the bleeding, but … in the delay, your father lost a lot of blood, Mr. Germaine. And with the entry point so close to one of his vertebrae, there could be some complications. It's too soon to tell."

"But will he live?" Vikkas pressed.

Dro held his breath, wishing he'd arrived sooner.

"Barring any unforeseen complications, but the next twenty-four hours are critical."

"Can I see him?" Vikkas asked.

She shook her head, her eyeglasses slipping a few inches down the bridge of her nose. "I'm sorry, but he's heavily sedated and will be out for the rest of the night. If his condition improves, you'll be able to see him first thing tomorrow. Once again, it'll be one at a time," she clarified. "You might as well go home and get some rest. Visiting hours begin at ten o'clock tomorrow morning."

"Understood," Vikkas said quietly, echoing the sadness of everyone in the room.

She squeezed his arm and promised to call him if there were any changes.

When she swept past the group and out of the room, Vikkas collapsed in a chair, his head in his hands. "If anything happens to him ..."

"It won't," Daron vowed.

"I'll call in some favors with our friends at the precinct," Shaz spoke up.

"No need for that," Daron said. "There'll be men watching him twenty-four hours a day. No one gets in his room but family and us."

Vikkas nodded. "Nothing can happen to him. There's so much left undone."

"It won't," Dro promised. "Why don't we take this conversation to The Castle? We have much to discuss and we shouldn't do it here."

CHAPTER 25

Sunrays peeked through the clouds as Kaleb drove around the bends of a sleepy area in Wilmette. The city boasted of manicured lawns and homes with modern architectural charm. Far enough away from the burned structures and old-school muscle cars of his old neighborhood, Kaleb felt as though he could breathe easy.

Breezing through the grassy acreage moving toward The Castle, Kaleb inhaled the scent of fresh-cut grass as he lowered the window. His heartbeat took an uptick as he wondered how this meeting would go. Kaleb hadn't seen Khalil in over fifteen years and had ended a relationship with the only positive male role model he had in his life with a call telling him that he wouldn't be returning to Macro Prep. He hadn't even been given the chance to provide Khalil any justification for the rushed decision.

Kaleb drove into a driveway that was the length of the entire front of The Castle. The majestic, sandstone structure featured two-story leaded glass windows on all sides and stately turrets. Kaleb was impressed, thinking that an ordinary family couldn't have lived there at any time—a castle of this sort is where one would find kings and queens, not everyday people. A quick scan of the parking spaces showed that he had arrived before the others, but Khalil's legendary roadster was parked along with several other cars, one of those vehicles was a Wilmette

Police Department Cruiser. Yellow caution tape crossed the opening of the estate; an ominous sign.

Jogging the length of the space from his car to the entrance, Kaleb quickly moved to the castle's vaulted entrance. He thought about the word Zephyr used to describe his home—"cozy". Zephyr's place looked like a miniature version of the building he was now approaching.

Though Wilmette was a nice little distance from South Shore, Kaleb hadn't made it his business to visit any city near his hometown until Reno put an offer on the table. The caution tape stretched across the entrance was a stark reminder of why even a day trip was not in his best interest. However, the projects Reno had slated to work on in the Chatham and South Shore neighborhoods intrigued Kaleb, despite the potential dangers. He rarely thought about his former life, but it was all he could think about when yesterday's secret visit had him riding through his old gang territory. One cruise down Halsted resulted in a migraine and a cold sweat after he saw someone who reminded him of J-Killa, a rival leader.

Casting all other thoughts aside, Kaleb bent under the yellow plastic barrier and eased his way to the Castle's open front door. He recalled one of the few conversations that Khalil had with him, mentioning a family castle. Kaleb had enjoyed the talk, believing his mentor was fantasizing about big things in life. Khalil had always been encouraging that way. He thought about the efforts Khalil made to take him under his wing, and show him a better life than the rumors told, but anger about his father's death had consumed his thoughts and strained all of his interactions.

Kaleb glanced over his shoulder, taking a glimpse at all of the cars that were parked in the lot, wondering if the police had gathered any clues that would tell them who had committed the crime. For a brief moment, he also wondered if he should fill Reno in on a few details that he wasn't aware of.

Stepping close to the threshold, Kaleb was surprised at the sound of deep, echoed murmuring. His heart jumped into his throat with one glance to spots that looked like blood spatter, something he'd seen too much of growing up on the block of his old neighborhood.

Following the voices that bounced off the stone interior walls, Kaleb moved steadily, without hurrying, to the source of the noise. Surveying his surroundings, he took note of the large rooms and ornate fixtures that adorned the tables and walls, being careful not to touch anything.

Who on earth would try to kill a man as honorable as Khalil Germaine? And why did one of his so-called "brothers" believe Kaleb had something to do with it?

CHAPTER 26

The man at the horseshoe end of the semi-circular conference table was a carbon copy of his father. But for his midnight-black hair, minus that shock of silver in his widow's peak, Shaz would have believed Khalil was sitting with them. One thing was clear, while Khalil Germaine was the visionary and spiritual leader, Vikkas Germaine was all business.

After Crystal, Vikkas' newly-hired assistant, led them through a winding underground corridor, she ushered them into the circular, state-of-the-art conference room where coffee, tea, juice, and delicate sandwiches graced a wooden credenza, Vikkas invited them to enjoy the refreshments. A glance around the room had Shaz wondering what kind of equipment lay behind several wooden doors decorated with ornate handles.

Aside from Vikkas, seven other men stood around the room. Shaz knew four of them. Two were strangers he'd seen at the hospital on his way out after seeing Khalil—the one connection they had in common. The arctic blast of the air conditioning almost made him shiver. He was about to check the vibration from his phone when Khalil's lookalike spoke.

"Gentlemen, please take a seat." His tone was low but commanding as if he was used to arresting people simply with his words.

Jai and Reno ended their conversation, pulled out two navy executive chairs, and sat next to each other. Dro and Grant abandoned their drinks on the sideboard and took their seats. The newcomers—Kaleb and Daron—scanned the men before Kaleb claimed the empty space next to Reno. Shaz silenced his phone.

"Has anyone managed to raise Dwayne?" Jai asked, putting a pointed look on Shaz, who had been the closest to him in high school.

"Not a peep. Text, email, a phone call—he hasn't responded to anything," Grant said, crossing one slack-covered leg over the other.

"Or anyone," Reno chimed in. "I've tried too."

"And then there were … eight," Vikkas said, the weariness in his voice unmistakable.

Everybody's attention went to Vikkas, who'd only brought a tablet into the room with him. His calm demeanor belied the life-threatening experience he'd been through with his father. A silk royal-blue tie sat snug inside a well-cut charcoal suit that probably cost an arm and a leg. Shaz knew this because he favored high-end suits as well.

"There were wrongs that my father wanted to make right. He considered all of you to be 'King material.' My father asked me to chair this meeting, hoping you would understand the depth of what he requested and accept his offer. I know some of you grew up together, but let's start by introducing ourselves," he said. "For those who don't know me, I am Vikkas Germaine."

He pointed to Daron. "Let's start with you."

Each man gave his name and a summary of what he did for a living. When it was his turn, Shaz shared that he specialized in family immigration and did some voluntary work connected to his business. The meeting felt like high drama and cloak-and-dagger business, but he respected Khalil too much not to be here. He'd been shocked when he finally laid eyes on Khalil. The man was as pale as the sheets he lay on inside the intensive care unit.

When Khalil opened his eyes and welcomed him, Shaz had been relieved. His mentor's voice was much stronger than expected. Given the situation, Shaz held on to his questions. In a few sentences, Khalil revealed his involvement in The Castle, and where he had been shot. Shaz was impressed because of the property's reputation and its exclusive clientele made up of tycoons and celebrities. Other than telling Shaz he had an assignment for him and his magnet school brothers within the organization, Khalil had revealed nothing else, leaving that to his son.

Vikkas' voice cut into Shaz's straying thoughts. "I'm sure you're wondering what exactly is expected of you, but bear with me."

A beep came from the cell on the table in front of him, and Vikkas scanned their faces. "Give me a moment, please. This is important."

Shaz's mind went back to the hospital visit with Khalil. He left the place mystified but expecting to be fully clued in by the confidential document Khalil asked him to study before this meeting. The envelope arrived yesterday evening, which hadn't allowed him much time. Given the fact that Shaz partly owed his success to Khalil, he'd done what his mentor asked. Now, he honed in on the three men he'd just met, wondering what their role would be in all this. He had a host of questions, but those could wait. First, he needed to know exactly what he was getting himself into. Guilt pricked him again over ignoring the information Khalil had sent and the first request he made four weeks ago.

Vikkas pressed a button on a specialized remote. A pair of cherry wood doors slid open to reveal a huge flat-screen television anchored to a recessed wall. The property Shaz had only been vaguely aware of, and in which they now sat, appeared on the screen. "Gentlemen, The Castle and its restructuring will be the focus of this first meeting."

The men shuffled, and Shaz and Dro exchanged a glance before their gazes returned to the screen, where the sprawling property was still displayed.

Vikkas gave them a whirlwind virtual tour of the premises, which to Shaz's surprise housed not only an exclusive community, but a holistic clinic, gaming lounges, several gyms, a mega-exclusive gentleman's club, and a ladies' circle. Hearing about all the undisclosed businesses patronized by the rich and famous piqued his interest.

"A physical tour will reveal the scope and expanse of The Castle and all that's contained within this property. We'll do that after this meeting."

His gaze rested on each man momentarily. "Any questions so far?"

Shaz had a thousand and he saw it in his brothers' expressions, and Daron and Kaleb's faces as well, but it was as if they were in one accord—they'd wait until they had more information. Each man either voiced a 'no' or shook his head. Their gazes, pinned to Vikkas, were a clue they were waiting for him to get to the details that would alter their lives substantially.

Vikkas was like a puppeteer. With one click, the screen was again concealed behind the double doors. The silence was complete. Not even the air-conditioning dared to spew a sound into the room.

"My father has owned this property for some time, constructing the rest of these buildings around a small bridge that existed for nearly one-hundred years. What it has become is far from his original vision. He wants to change that." After a couple of beats during which he scanned their faces, he added, "That's where you come in. He always knew you had the courage, integrity, and strength to complement and complete his vision for The Castle."

In five minutes, he outlined how The Castle had shifted from an incubator of dreams to a den of iniquity. "The Castle has maintained its reputation for those looking in from the outside. But my father discovered some ... let's say, under-the-radar member activities that made him start delving further into the transactions related to The Castle, its subsidiaries, and offshore holdings. That's what made someone want to end his life and mine."

The restlessness in the conference room was muted, but obvious. A range of expressions crossed the men's faces, from unease to anxiety to anger. Shaz had a bunch of conflicting emotions of his own. Who would be bold enough to try to kill Khalil, and was he down for taking on whatever part he was supposed to play?

As he listened, Shaz's heart rate quickened. The heaviness in his gut told him there was more under the surface of the document he'd been fed. While it detailed the development of the property and the homes, businesses, and recreational facilities on site, he'd felt something was missing while he was reading.

This was it.

Vikkas' voice pulled Shaz out of his thoughts. "My father has seen fit to appoint the group of you as Kings of the Castle, so to speak. Previously, my father allowed the members with the biggest stake to have a say in the general operations and to guide the direction of The Castle, its purpose, and financial holdings and properties. That's about to change." He opened a leather folder and brought an iPad to life. "What he requires of you is first that you accept the appointment as managing partner, which puts you all on a higher standing than any current member. Second, that you sign a confidentiality clause, and third, that you recognize what happens in The Castle stays in The Castle." A faint smile crossed his face. "Sort of like Vegas, but more like …"

"Reno," the brothers supplied, except Daron and Kaleb, who exchanged a curious glance.

"He had the confidence you'd be all-in, because of his history with you and what he had charged you to do when you graduated."

A collective sound of acknowledgment came from the group, and once again, Shaz wondered about the men he didn't know as well as the others. Were they Khalil's students, as well? How did they fit into the scheme of things?

"Do we have time to think about any of this?" Jai asked.

"That was going to be my question," Grant added.

"You had time to do that while you were reading that confidential file," Vikkas said, not bothering to hide his disdain.

"What are the risks?" Daron picked up his hat and stroked the edge of the brim.

Tapping his pen against the table, Vikkas said, "We have world-class safety systems on-site—"

"Yet someone shot Khalil, didn't they, and barely missed you?" Daron countered.

Vikkas inhaled, and there was a momentary slip of his normal range of calm. "Yes, but under extraordinary circumstances. Trust me when I say this lapse has been taken care of and won't happen again. My father somehow put you." He glanced at Daron. "In charge of that without checking with me first."

"Will this appointment preclude any of the projects we all have going on now?" Shaz asked, frowning as he thought of having to take leave of his clients and the time-consuming work involved in keeping families together. "Businesswise, I mean."

"If anything, being associated with The Castle will enhance what you do."

That didn't answer his question. Besides, he didn't need more business. As things stood, he was overburdened half the time. He'd do anything for Khalil, but his clients also needed him. And that work had a humanitarian aspect as well. One of the major tenets of learning that Khalil had instilled in all of them.

"What else is there?" Shaz asked. He'd always been one to question everything and find all the angles, which made him good at his studies and in his chosen field.

Dro, Jai, Grant, and Reno frowned at Shaz, but then their gaze went to Vikkas as if they, too, expected something more.

After studying Shaz for a few seconds, Vikkas' focus went back to his tablet. He cleared his throat, then announced, "My father wants you to work together to restructure the operations of The Castle, but I'd like to put something else on the plate."

Everyone's gaze shifted to him.

"We need to find out who tried to kill him."

CHAPTER 27

"I know this is dangerous territory, but can you contact any of your old buddies from your banging days?" Reno asked Kaleb, moving away from the group congregated outside of the conference room, shutting the door behind them, leaving the other men in their own conversation as they took a short break.

Kaleb gripped the back of the leather chair and placed a smoldering glare on Reno. "Do you know what you're asking of me?"

Reno nodded, knowing this was a big query. "I just received an update from Skyler at the shelter. Zuri is a new client. Her father and fiancé are in Chicago searching for her and it's not a good thing."

Zuri Okusanya had been in the States for five years, getting a degree in International Relations, only returning to Tanzania to celebrate her mother's home-going. Her father forbade her to return to the States and demanded that she take her rightful place as Djimon's wife, securing her future and the family's finances since the Aku family pledged $200,000 as a dowry. The insult caused by her disappearance could only be rectified by two things—her compliance or her death.

Reno shook his head in disbelief as he relayed the information to his friend. "She didn't want an arranged marriage, and her father accused her of letting the Western world strip Zuri of her culture."

"Sounds like the movie *Coming to America*." Kaleb grinned, but Reno didn't crack a smile.

"In addition to that, the Sovereign Kings are snooping around the transitional housing apartments," Reno said, perching on the circular boardroom table. "I don't know if they're casing the place for a new stash spot for drugs or if her father has some connections here. Either way, their increased presence is putting all the women I'm protecting at risk. I had no choice but to move them."

"This is serious," Kaleb said, and this time there wasn't a trace of a smile or smirk on his face.

"All I need is information, and you're in a better position to get it than I am. I mean——" Reno stepped back and gestured to his face. "Who's gonna talk to this straight-laced pretty Italian boy?"

"True dat." Kaleb lightly chuckled, giving his friend a fist bump. "Once upon a time, I wouldn't have flinched at the idea of administering street justice to these young punks." He pulled out the chair and took a seat, then Reno followed suit.

Reno placed a hand on Kaleb's broad shoulder. "It shouldn't have to go that far, but I'm confident you could handle that business."

"All jokes aside, there's a reason why my family was uprooted to Detroit." Lowering his voice as the other men filtered back in, giving them a suspicious look, Kaleb whispered, "To protect my mother, I turned state's evidence against the leader of the gang. In return, I was granted immunity from prosecution and relocated. This week is the first time I've set foot in Chicago in fifteen years." Kaleb paused, cracking his knuckles. "Ain't no love for a snitch in the hood, but there are long memories. Evidently, one of your friends has one."

"Damn, KV. I thought your mother found a better paying job, and that's why y'all had to move." He ran a hand through his hair. "I guess that was your cover story?"

"I couldn't say anything," Kaleb replied, shifting so the leather chair sighed under his movement. "Truthfully, I wasn't supposed to keep in touch with anyone from my past. I saved your number in my new phone under the name Mariah and shuffled the area code around, so my mother didn't recognize that it was a Chicago number."

"That's extreme, but I understand." Reno eyed Kaleb with a clearer appreciation of the value of their continued friendship, one the other kings weren't aware of. "I'll find another way."

"Your girl needs help," Kaleb shot back, bumping Reno's shoulder with his fist. "The kind a straight-laced pretty boy from Chatham can't provide."

"Zuri isn't my girl," Reno protested a little too loudly, scanning the conference room to make sure the other men hadn't overheard his mini outburst. "She's a client."

Kaleb gave him the side-eye, and a half-smile. "But you care about her, right?"

"On second thought, let's table this entirely," he replied, matching Kaleb's intense stare. "Interacting with your old gang is one thing, but sniffing around them when a bounty might still be on your head is a risk that's not worth taking."

"Agreed. We'll figure something else out, but you didn't answer my question about Zuri."

Reno grinned, clapping a hand on Kaleb's shoulder. "I didn't, did I?"

CHAPTER 28

The meeting ended with a new agenda on the table, and a date for all of the paperwork to be signed giving the men access complete rights, privileges and co-ownership of The Castle and all of its financial holdings and properties.

Jai glanced at the one empty seat that remained at the table. "We need to go see about Dwayne."

"Why? He's made it painfully obvious he wants no parts of this," Kaleb said, placing his palms on the table. "So why would we even want him along for this ride?"

"There's an empty seat at this table," Shaz said, gathering up the final documents and tucking them under his arm. "There's a purpose for each of us."

"If we accept it," Vikkas interjected.

"Have you?" Reno shot back, almost glaring at him. "Why weren't you here running things? You had to have known how bad it was."

"My place was with my father," Vikkas countered. "I don't have any regrets about helping with his work."

"And you didn't get *any* vibe that these dudes were going rogue?" Daron asked, swiveling in the leather chair to face Vikkas. "None at all, huh?"

"Too trusting," Kaleb mumbled.

"Hey, you can't say too much about trust," Grant said, glaring at

Kaleb. "The only reason we're giving you a pass is because Reno went in on us at the hospital."

"Let's not go back down that road," Vikkas warned before putting his focus on Daron and Reno. "I had suggested that I remain here, run things, but my father insisted that I be with him, wanting to make up for the times he spent babysitting other people's children and neglecting his own."

The unspoken accusation that "other people's children" meant the majority of the men in this room was not lost on anyone.

"Yes, he seemed to take a special liking to Jai," Reno said, shifting his gaze to the man sitting next to Grant. "Must've been that whole East Indian thing."

Shaz frowned, perching on the table. "Or the fact that they both have that same shock of silver hair at the widow's peak …"

All gazes shifted to Jai, who grimaced under the intense scrutiny.

"Brethren, we're getting off track here," Grant said, but he still had his eyes on Jai. "There are more things that bind us than separate us. We're going to have enough hitting us without us tearing down a new foundation before it's even built."

"He's right," Vikkas said, but a slight edge of concern tinged his expression, and he, too, kept his focus on Jai far longer than it seemed warranted. "One accord. Khalil chose each of you for a reason."

"He chose Dwayne, too," Daron offered. "We should at least attempt to get a handle on him before we proceed."

"And I have a bit of a crisis," Kaleb said. "I was supposed to return to Detroit, but tonight the police are taking a look into a recent chain of events surrounding one of my properties. And I have to stick around."

Vikkas nodded. "We've got you. No worries. Daron, do you have an address for Dwayne?"

Jai rattled off the information before Daron could reach for his phone. Everyone paused, but Jai shrugged. "I had a little intel on all of you before I arrived. Had to see what I was walking into."

"That's fair," Daron said, moving his hands from his pocket and back to the table.

Jai took a long sip of Amaretto liqueur. "But now that we're on the subject ... two of you all are like ghosts."

"And they might want to keep it that way," Daron said, effectively shutting down that discussion as Shaz signaled to Jai to pour him a shot. "Dwayne, people."

"I say," Shaz said accepting the tumbler with a nod of thanks. "Confront him man to man, and see what shakes down."

"I'm game" Reno went to the bar to grab his own drink.

Grant lifted his glass in salute. "Me too."

"I have work to do," Kaleb said, parking his long-limbed form back into the leather chair. "I'm not in the habit of fighting a battle someone doesn't want us to win."

"Running already, eh?" Jai said, giving him a sly smile. "Sounds familiar."

Kaleb flipped him the bird.

"Fellas, let's keep it civil," Daron said, but there was a slight expression of appreciation that signaled he was all right with Kaleb's show of bravado.

"I'll be civil when they are," Kaleb shot back. "Despite what any of you think, you come for me, I give you exactly what you ask for."

"On that note," Shaz stood and sighed. "Who's driving to Dwayne's?"

"I'll roll with Reno and Vikkas," Grant said.

Daron chimed in, "I'll be taking my own vehicle."

"I've always wanted to test out a Tesla," Jai said. "Can I take it for a spin?

"You want to keep breathing?" Daron shot back.

"Ouch." Jai shrugged. "Can't separate a man and his machine."

Vikkas slid a silver passkey across the table to Kaleb. "First level. South Shore wing. We'll see you when we get back."

The men collected their envelopes and filed toward the door, leaving Kaleb at the table alone.

"On second thought ..." Kaleb stood and sprinted to catch up. "I'm rolling with y'all."

CHAPTER 29

DWAYNE HARPER

"More than half a dozen men in business suits are at the front door," Val said to her twin brother, Dwayne, as she stepped out onto the patio of his South Holland home. "Do you know who they are?"

"Yep." Dwayne reached into the smoker, pulled out a piping hot brisket, and placed it on a platter. He used a fork and pulled off a bite to offer to his sister.

Val blew on the steaming morsel, then placed it in her mouth. Her eyes rolled upward as she tasted it. She relished all the effort he took to make it the best barbecue on this side of the globe. She gave her brother a thumbs-up, then asked, "Were you expecting those men to stop by?"

"Kind of," he answered, picking up the platter and giving her his back to ponder.

"So I should let them in?"

"Absolutely not." His voice was calm but firm, signaling that his answer was non-negotiable. Walking through the sliding glass door with his sister trailing behind him, he added, "They're from The Castle."

He glanced over his shoulder in time to see her eyes light up. He was getting so many calls, texts, and emails all of a sudden, the family had teased him about taking on an illegal job. He fessed up and told them about The Castle, and now he wished that he hadn't. They were thrilled that he'd been invited to become part of such a prestigious group. But no matter how much they encouraged him to take that step, something didn't sit right with him. "They don't have anything to say that I want to hear."

Val frowned and narrowed her eyes at him. "Okay, I'll let you handle this."

Uncle Bubba met them at the entrance to the dining room. Val gave him a peck on his weathered cheek and scurried past him. "I smell my macaroni and cheese. I'd better go check on it before it's on the wrong side of done." She rushed toward the adjoining kitchen.

"Wait, take this with you," he said to Val as he reached out to take the brisket from his nephew. "Keep it warm for a few minutes."

When she left the room, Uncle Bubba said, "Some men are here to see you, Dwayne. Said they needed to talk to you 'bout The Castle."

Dwayne scrubbed his hands down his face and sighed. "I know who they are, Uncle Bubba, and what they want to talk to me about." He slid several plates out of the china cabinet and walked around the table placing them in front of each chair. "But I'm not interested."

"Aw, come on, Dwayne. Just hear them out," he insisted. "Besides, I already invited them in. I told them to wait in the livin' room. It would be rude for me to throw 'em out on the street for no reason."

"I've got plenty reason." Dwayne turned and made two steps toward the living room before Uncle Bubba caught him by his upper arm.

"It won't hurt you to listen one mo' time." He released his hold on Dwayne's arm and nodded toward the table.

Dwayne pinched the bridge of his nose and blew out a breath of frustration as he took a seat and watched Uncle Bubba head into the living room to get the men he hadn't laid eyes on since his high school days at Macro.

Each one of them greeted him, embracing him as though they were long-lost brothers. Two of them he didn't recognize. All of them, dressed in suits that cost more than he made in an entire month, looked like brand-new money. They were casket-sharp as Uncle Bubba would say.

They claimed seats around the dining room table and each gave Dwayne a condensed version of what was in store at The Castle and how much they wanted him to be with them. Dwayne absorbed every word and then gave a pointed look to each of the eight men sitting around the table. "Sounds good and all, but I'm going to stay in my lane."

The men looked at each other and rose from the table. One by one, they extended a hand to him, and offered a parting embrace.

"I sure hope you give this some more thought, brother," Daron said as he snatched his hat off a nearby buffet table and placed it on his head.

"Don't let no be your final answer," Reno added. "You might not see it this way yet, but you need us just as much as we need you. It would be a win-win if you join us."

The swinging door to the kitchen opened. Val, along with Dwayne's girlfriend, Tiffany, came into the dining room. Hands covered in oven mitts held bowls of food that were so succulent that even the lids on top of them couldn't mask the delicious scents escaping into the room. Both women stared at the impressive group of men.

"Pick your mouth up off the floor, Tiffany," Dwayne warned, practically growling. "You too, Val."

The women sprang to life and their welcoming smiles bestowed on the unwanted guests caused Dwayne to bristle.

Dwayne gave the men a dismissive wave. "We're getting ready for our family meal. You can see your way out."

"Have some manners," Tiffany scolded, setting her bowl down and going back into the kitchen.

"Have a good evening, gentlemen," Val said, giving Dwayne the evil eye as she placed her bowl on the table, rounded the table, and stood near the entryway. "I'll show you to the door."

Tiffany returned with a tray holding two more dishes.

"Wait. Are those collards?" Shaz asked, peering over Dwayne's shoulder and into the bowl Tiffany sat on the table. He glanced at Val, gave her a conspirator's wink. She smiled and went to the table.

"It sure is. And it's sitting right next to the best-looking mac and cheese I've seen in a while," Reno chimed in when Val removed the foil from the rectangular dish she had placed on the table.

"Brisket too," Grant and Daron chorused as Tiffany took one of the dishes off her tray.

Jai inhaled and let it out slowly. "And sweet potato pie. I'd know that scent anywhere."

Val tried to stifle her laughter and so did her husband, Hunter, who came from the upstairs bedroom and stood next Tiffany.

"We don't need no help identifyin' the food," Uncle Bubba teased, picking up a plate and filling it as he tried to hide a grin.

Dwayne glared, first at the men, then at his family, knowing that they were in cahoots in trying to change his mind.

"Gentlemen, would you care to join us for dinner?" Val said, causing Dwayne to nearly choke.

Kaleb was out of his blazer in a jiffy. Shaz, Grant, and Reno all followed suit.

Vikkas slid his tie over his shoulder and said, "Thought you'd never ask."

"Great," Tiffany said, rubbing her hands together then signaling Hunter to grab the extra chairs. "The bathroom's just down that hall." She blew an air kiss Dwayne's way as the men filed into the bathroom to wash their hands. When they all returned to the dinner table, Uncle Bubba teased, "And look at 'em, all civilized and whatnot. Where'd you find these men? On Giggle?"

"It's Google, Uncle Bubba," Dwayne said dryly.

"You know what I meant."

CHAPTER 30

"Why is she here?" Varsha Germaine demanded the moment Vikkas and Milan stepped into the private hospital waiting room.

An array of family members from the Germaine, Gupta, Bhandari, and Maharaj families turned their attention toward Milan. Most of them had arrived from New Dehli a few hours ago.

"Dad specifically requested her presence," Vikkas explained to his mother. "She is my guest and his."

Varsha gave Milan a disdainful once-over that put a distinct chill in the air. "Well, just as long as she knows her place."

Vikkas stiffened. "Her place?"

Milan's hand gripped his upper arm, but he ignored that warning.

"Her place is by my side," he confirmed, putting an arm around Milan's waist and pulling her even closer. "And this is not the time or place to have a conversation that'll be unpleasant for all of us."

Varsha placed a multi-ringed hand over her heart. "What are you saying? Uncle Nayan has taken care of arranging everything since your father has been unwilling to move forward."

"My father supports my choice one-hundred percent," Vikkas said, taking Milan's hand in his and giving his mother a speaking glare that said she was dangerously close to crossing a line. "He recognizes that some things do not need to follow tradition. And I will marry for love or not at all."

"You are not going to marry this ... this ... " She shivered as though the word she would use to describe Milan disgusted her. "You *will* consent to a marriage with one of the Gupta sisters."

"Mama, I told you I would give it a thought for the twentieth time, and give you another answer when I was ready," he countered. "Now I'm ready—again. And the answer is still no. I am not marrying a woman of your choosing. Father was bound to his family that way, and he wants me to have options that he did not."

Milan tugged at his sleeve. "Vikkas, I'm not getting in the middle of your family drama. Why don't you call me after you get all of this straightened out?"

She extracted from his hold, grabbed her tote and was near the threshold before he could formulate his next words.

"Milan, I will say this," he began and she paused, turning just enough for her dark brown eyes to lock on his. "There's a lot you don't know about me and there's a lot we have to learn about each other." He moved in so there was only a hairsbreadth of space between them. "But the one thing I'm not about is chaos and disorder. Would I bring you back into my life if I didn't have my affairs in order? I've been saying no to this for half of my entire life."

"Well, what is your mother all in an uproar about?" she asked, taking in the crowd who had ended all other conversations to focus on the drama unfolding in the waiting room.

"They are talking about what they *hope* will happen because their biological clock is ticking loud enough for everyone to hear. You and I," he gestured between them with an index finger. "That's a promise. I haven't agreed in all this time and they were so sure that I would give in that they're breaking that poor woman's heart by planning a wedding I have no intention of attending. Except as a guest. Father didn't spend one red cent. Nor did he make any promises on my behalf," Vikkas admitted, causing his mother to avert her gaze to Uncle Nayan, who had been the main cheerleader of a Gupta-Germaine union because of their massive wealth and connections in India that would benefit him personally. Khalil never had such designs. He always said that money is not the path to happiness, and he learned that firsthand when he landed a woman who had a selfish and unforgiving heart as a wife.

"I love you, Mama," Vikkas said, placing a calming hand over the older woman's trembling one. "But you went too far on this one. Milan is the only woman I want in my life and that won't change. To be honest, it never changed despite how you or anyone felt about her. And none of it will matter to me. You don't have to accept her, but I have to love her—and that is what will matter to her."

Soon the families erupted in angry discourse so disruptive that the nurses came in to address the level of noise.

"Indian men are for Indian women," Uncle Nayan growled, his tone resolute. "Why can you not understand that? Our children come here and lose their culture, taking on American ways and women who have no true culture of their own."

Varsha sobbed, and the dramatics behind it brought all of the women over to console her. "You will break my heart if you take this girl to wife," she said in a wavering voice. "Sleep with her if you must, but—"

"Mama, stop right there," Vikkas said through his teeth. "I will not allow you to insult Milan that way."

"I am being truthful." She lifted her chin, meeting his gaze head on, emboldened by the family's support. "Their types are—"

"Not. One. More. Word," he said through his teeth.

The people in the room became eerily silent. All movements came to an abrupt halt.

Varsha parted her lips to speak.

"Mama. Stand down," his sister, Prisha warned, placing a hold on Milan's shoulder before pulling her into a warm embrace which Milan hesitantly returned. "This is one battle you are *never* going to win."

Varsha huffed, put a quick glance to Uncle Nayan, who threw up his hand, then to the Gupta men whose anger was so tangible it nearly filled the room.

"You owe Milan an apology," Vikkas said and she stiffened.

"I will not—"

"Not just for the insulting words today but all those years ago," Vikkas continued. "Apologize."

"That's not necessary," Milan whispered, but Vikkas gave her a look that persuaded her to allow this to happen.

Varsha fumbled with the material of her sari. "I am sorry if my words were unkind."

"If?" Vikkas hedged.

She grimaced and grumbles of discontent rippled through the room. "I am sorry that my words to you were unkind."

Milan didn't get a chance to respond before he took her hand and said, "Come, let's see about my father," he said. "One parent disowning me today is enough."

She gave his hand a squeeze, looking up at him, seemingly searching for signs that he was humoring her. "Your father wouldn't do that."

"You didn't hear him earlier," Vikkas replied, planting a kiss on her temple. "If he could've gotten out of that bed, he would've pushed me out the window if I hadn't heeded his advice to seek you out."

Milan smiled. "I said it before and I'll say it again—I always liked that man."

CHAPTER 31

The impromptu date to make up for his disapperance earlier that morning didn't quite start off the way Daron expected. Cameron had gifted him seven suits with Kevlar lining. He hadn't even commented on the fact that the new suits also had the special pockets used to store his devices. The woman was nothing short of phenomenal and he didn't want anything to come between them. If Katara's public statement about the decoy keychain tracker killed the curiosity and caused the story to die, then his company would become a distant memory and all would be well.

Cameron lightly bumped him with her hip, bringing his attention back to her. Daron smiled as they continued their walk away from The Hancock Center that housed The Signature room on the 95th floor, where they'd had dinner. His eyes roamed over Cameron's short black dress that made her sculpted legs seem miles long in her stilettos.

"Let's stop in here for a quick second." Daron tugged her toward the Cheesecake Factory.

Cameron looked at him as if he lost his mind. "We just ate."

He pulled her into his arms, holding her close. "I have every plan to work off all we consumed and figured we'd need a couple of cheesecake slices or something to replenish our energy." Daron planted a kiss on her cheek.

"Good, 'cause I made a visit to a specialty shop." Cameron slid her hand over his ass and gave it a squeeze. "You're in for a treat tonight. One of these days I'm going to upgrade you to handcuffs."

"When you agree to make this thing we have official, I'll consider it." Daron's hand glided over her round hip. He was tempted to skip the treats run and head straight home.

"You don't trust me." She pushed away from the embrace and gave him a playful scowl as they entered the crowded restaurant.

He had to choose his words carefully or all the lightheartedness would exit with a swiftness. "Babe, can I cuff you?"

"Hell no." She chuckled, stepping into the line.

"Why's that?" He smiled, nibbling her neck. "You don't trust me?"

"I don't want to have to become an escape artist when your phone rings and you disengage." She gently shoved him in the shoulder.

He frowned. Any time she was in his bed he had a hard time leaving. The morning Katara had called had been the exception. "I've never answered the phone in the midst of …"

"But you have no problems a few seconds after." She raised her eyebrows as if she was daring him to challenge that statement. "This isn't about me. It's about you."

"I'm dating a woman who's very guarded." Daron wrapped his arm around her waist. "And refuses to be an exclusive couple. Makes me wonder if we have issues that I should be concerned about."

"You think those issues would cause me to leave you cuffed to the bed?" Cameron threw him a narrowed gaze over her shoulder as if she was insulted.

Daron ignored the curious glance the red-haired cashier sent their way, and placed the dessert order, then moved away before responding, "Why do I feel like this went from a topic you tease me about to something I need to do to prove a point to you?"

Cameron remained silent, but those dark brown eyes were flashing with the efforts to keep her thoughts to herself. She gestured to the counter. "The cheesecakes are up."

He grabbed the bag and they made their way back to his Jag. Cameron brushed the strands of hair the warm breeze blew in her face behind her ear as they passed three guys heading north in the direction of the Hancock Building. They glanced in Cameron's direction then suddenly turned back, seemingly aiming for the parking garage. Daron unbuttoned his suit jacket, hoping he was being paranoid.

He could feel Cameron's body stiffen before she pivoted in the opposite way of where they were heading.

"Gentleman, are you lost?" Cameron slipped a hand into her purse.

"We found who we're looking for," the tallest of the three men replied but his focus was on Daron. "We saw you with Vikkas Germaine. We're only going to warn you once. We will not tolerate your interference with our business."

Daron stepped in front of Cameron, finally recognizing the man speaking as one that Vikkas had brought up in The Castle meeting. The only opportunity they would've had to see him with Vikkas was when the men left the hospital and held that first Castle meeting. "What I do or don't do is none of your business." He wrapped an arm around Cameron to hold her back.

The leader of the pack stepped forward, nodding toward Cameron. "You should concentrate on protecting her."

Daron eased his jacket back, showing them he was armed. "I suggest you walk away while you still can."

"You think you're big and bad enough to take us?" He glanced back at the other two smirking men standing behind him.

Cameron was ready to have his back. That little black dress and stilettos could fool anyone, but he was well aware of what his woman was capable of. Daron slid the keys out the jacket pocket and slipped them into her hand, along with the food. "Babe, please get in the car."

"Not happening." She flashed the weapon in her hand.

The man inched back, eyes widened when Cameron shifted and had him within the crosshairs. "Don't worry. We gave the message we wanted." He turned and motioned for the other two to leave. "It will only be trouble if he doesn't heed it."

Daron watched them walk away, then leveled his anger at Cameron. "Next time I tell you to get in the car ..." He grabbed the keys and moved toward the car. "Get in the damn car."

"Whoa." Cameron glared at him as he swung open the passenger door. "That's not how I roll." She slid into the seat and huffed.

"It is now." Daron closed her door then scanned the area before sliding behind the steering wheel. He cut his eyes over to her. Cameron's lips were squeezed together, her eyes narrowed as she glanced over at him. Then she turned and stared out the window.

Daron was pretty sure Cameron thought this incident was about the tracking device she had asked him to turn over to a government agency instead of cultivating it himself. "Cam, part of our new life means I look after you. You only use those skills when they are absolutely necessary."

"What if they were needed tonight?" She buckled up. "Three to one odds."

He took a few extra turns to make sure they weren't being followed. Daron made a mental note to text Steve to find out if Vikkas was being tailed and to review the drone footage from The Castle visits. "Do you remember before when you asked me not to—"

Cameron's head snapped toward him. "You're not about to bring up the time when I was undercover in your organization."

Daron merged into the traffic on Lake Shore Drive. "It's the same. You didn't want any distractions."

"I'm not ..."

"You are for me." Daron pressed the brakes as they hit a red light near Navy Pier. He glanced at her. "You're my queen and your safety comes first."

She pursed those red lips. "Okay, my King, but we're not typical people."

"Here's the new rules of engagement. If we're a team, we have each other's back." He refrained from using the word *couple* as the traffic surged forward. Daron accepted the reality that between his aunt and The Castle business, the craziness had probably just begun and that his relationship with Cameron was about to be tested to the max.

"No side-lining me," she warned. "But let me be clear, I don't need you to protect me."

Daron understood that watching after people was second nature to her. This was her time for someone to look after her and he didn't want this hiccup in his life to cause him to lose the ground he'd finally established. "I need you to be my woman, not my bodyguard."

"Daron, I don't mind letting you lead but you have to trust me to have your six." Cameron placed her hand over the arm resting on the console. "If I'm going down, I'd rather do it fighting than retreating."

"I'm trying not to put you in that position." He lifted her hand to his lips and planted a kiss on her soft skin.

"The last man that didn't trust me to help almost got me killed." She glared at him. "Try not to do the same."

CHAPTER 32

Kaleb left the grounds of The Castle and arrived at the 6th Precinct, his heart still pounding from the encounter with the men who felt he had no place among them, all while wondering who would've burned the house he'd just purchased. He resisted the urge to drive by the place, even though it was only blocks away from the station. Kaleb glanced in every direction surrounding the car, feeling as though all eyes were on him as he parked and walked into the building.

Zephyr was right. I can't hide in plain sight here.

The aroma of coffee filled the air as Kaleb entered the doors of the precinct.

"Can I speak to Officer Washington?" Kaleb asked the intake officer.

"Just one minute, please." The brunette picked up a phone and made the request, then looked at Kaleb. "He'll be right with you."

Kaleb paced the floor until a middle-aged man dressed in dark slacks and a crisp white broadcloth shirt came toward him.

"I'm Officer Washington." Memories of a younger version of the man flashed when extended his hand to greet Kaleb. The officer's lackluster tone, his wide nose, and the scar under his eye helped Kaleb recognize him as one of the men who used to patrol the block he lived on as a child. He hoped the man didn't recognize him. Police often had long memories, too long for Kaleb's comfort. "How are you today, sir?"

"I'd be doing a lot better if I didn't have to deal with this issue," he responded, receiving Officer Washington's hand for a hearty shake.

"Understandable. Follow me."

Kaleb trailed through the crowded office filled with uniform-clad men and women swarming among other investigators and plain-clothed civilians. When they reached a desk in a private corner of the area. He took a seat in front of a well-organized desk and asked, "Do you have any idea who set my property on fire, Officer?"

Officer Washington opened a drawer at the side of the table and pulled out a manila folder. Laying it flat on the surface, he separated the contents and picked out a picture of a girl.

"Eliana Steed," the officer informed him as he locked his gaze on Kaleb.

Kaleb's eyebrows drew in as he examined the picture. A bronze-skinned girl with eyes that told a sad story looked back at him.

"Who is she?"

"That's what we'd like to know," the officer said, leveling an even more intense gaze on Kaleb. "She was caught running from the scene—a scene that has a few bodies attached to it."

Kaleb flinched at the officer's word. "Bodies?" he pressed, watching as the officer's face twisted as though he was the one who was confusion. "What are you talking about?"

"There were five other girls in the building, aged sixteen to nineteen years old. They didn't survive the fire. The neighbors reported seeing heavy traffic for a house that was basically abandoned."

Kaleb absorbed that information as well as the officer's critical tone. "I just purchased that house less than a month ago and started renovations last week."

"And you didn't notice anything or anybody strange at the site?" Officer Washington's forehead rippled as he gave Kaleb an incredulous stare.

"I live out of town, Officer," Kaleb explained, trying to hold his composure. *Bodies. Five bodies.* "I hired a company to start the project and they hadn't mentioned anything suspicious. I was scheduled to visit the site this week."

Officer Washington slid a notepad from his pocket. "What is your occupation, Mr. Valentine?"

"I'm a real estate developer in the Metro Detroit area."

"Can you account for your whereabouts the night of August 7th?"

Kaleb narrowed his gaze on the officer's heated and steely glare.

"I was in Detroit, Michigan on a yacht … cruising the Detroit River at a ceremony to receive another award for my company," Kaleb replied.

"And what's the reason you took a flight into Chicago late last night, then flew back early this morning?"

"Why?"

Officer Washington turned to his computer, glanced down at his notes, then tapped on the keyboard.

"What are you doing?" Kaleb questioned.

"I'm inputting your information and preparing the case, Mr. Valentine. As well as sharing some pertinent information with the Wilmette Police that might help with another case. I have just a few more questions."

"No, sir." Kaleb jumped up from the cracked vinyl chair. "I'm contacting my attorney. You won't be pinning any of these on me."

The officer stood, glared openly at Kaleb as he said, "Well, as the saying goes … don't leave town."

"Unless you're about to charge me," Kaleb began, straightening his jacket. "You can't hold me here."

"You're a rich man, Mr. Valentine," he shot back with a sneer. "Private jet trips twice between Chicago and Detroit within a twenty-four-hour period? That's awful suspicious." He dismissed Kalebe with a wave. "I'm sure you'll figure out your best movet."

CHAPTER 33

"I have a proposition for you."

Vikkas placed the office phone on the cradle, then turned the documents in his hand face-down and out of Nayan Maharaj's view. Shaz had sent them over earlier, and it was everything the nine men needed to complete the legal documents, transfers, and stock certificates. The one thing they all agreed on was vacating all current members and forcing the minor ones to reapply.

"And why would I listen to anything you have to say?" he asked, putting his focus on the stocky man.

"Because I know something you do not," Nayan replied, gesturing for three more men—dressed in full Indian garb—to follow him into the office. They settled in seats near the door as though they hadn't planned to stay long. With assessing eyes, they scanned the expansive space— marble tiles, cream walls, matching draperies, and one wall dedicated to a range of awards.

"There is a secret your family has been keeping from you for years," Nayan continued, sliding into a high-backed chair directly across from the desk. "Your real family."

"Uncle, it is best that you and your minions leave my office. Right now."

Nayan huffed, seemingly undeterred by Vikkas' tone. "You are about to let strangers take something that belongs to me."

Three of the men's heads whipped to Nayan, who quickly amended. "I—I mean, us. *We* should control the wealth of The Castle."

Vikkas swept a look across all of the men, finding that the other three still seemed unsettled by Nayan's words. "I notice you specifically say wealth and not the work and purpose—which is what brought the wealth you're so interested in. Your motivation has always been money. That has never been what drives my father."

"Your father turned his back on the family the minute he used his portion of the Maharaj fortune for something other than family endeavors."

"I'm curious." Vikkas steepled his fingers under his chin. "You're all up in my father's business. What did you do with your share of the money?"

Nayan visibly blanched. "That does not concern you."

"Oh, but it does," Vikkas countered, grinning at the flush of color that flooded the man's skin. "I'd like to know what your true motivation is all about."

Nayan grimaced, and his gaze shifted to the painting behind Vikkas. "The investments were sound. The people I placed them with were not."

"You squandered the money."

The men sitting near the door shared a speaking glance that Nayan didn't see because he had his back to them.

"I would not call it—"

"You squandered the money," Vikkas insisted and watched him squirm. "Now, you begrudge the fact that my father has not only brought in wealth effortlessly, but also managed to do the majority of what he set out to do." Vikkas shook his head. "How sad for you. But your failures have nothing to do with me."

"India has its own problems now," Nayan said causing the others to mumble their affirmation. "Rampant poverty, so much so, that people visit and tell others not to come. India needs wealth and stability. So many are focused on their own self-interests."

Vikkas coughed into his hands, trying not to laugh outright. Nayan was one to talk about self-interest, when that was all the man seemed to embrace.

"And if you comply with this request and assert your right to have The Castle holdings all under your control, we will restore your surname to Maharaj. Instead of that Anglo-French one, you now bear that is distant from your true culture."

Vikkas stood from behind the glass desk and moved until he was a few inches from Nayan, then perched on the edge. "Khalil took the basic tenets of a peaceful religion—gender equality, racial equality, service to humanity—and put them in a secular format for any and everyone to appreciate. That is something that transcends pure religion. That is humane."

Nayan glared and parted his lips to speak, but Vikkas held up a hand to silence him.

"He was on a spiritual journey in making sure that people who have been the most overlooked by society had a chance to build something of value. That is what makes him a great man."

Nayan's laughter echoed. "Great man? Spiritual man?" He slapped a hand to his knee. "Ha! Not so much. Human desires ruled him just like the rest of us." Nayan stood so he was at his full height that was still two feet shorter than Vikkas. "Why do you think he was so vested in having those particular men involved in his life? It is not a coincidence. He took that humanitarian aspect to an entirely different level." Nayan looked to Tehan whose silent disapproval was almost tangible. "Do you want to tell him or shall I?"

Tehan crossed one leg over the other. "One of those little bastards is Khalil's son."

He was silent for a moment to let Vikkas absorb that tidbit of information. The other two men exchanged a glance over the half-moon console table between them.

"This man has more claim to The Castle than you ever had. Keep that in mind."

The four men sauntered to the door, but it was Nayan who looked over his shoulder and said, "When you are ready to listen to reason, I will be here. In the meantime, do not let those men sign the papers. You will regret it."

CHAPTER 34

Shaz winced and squeezed his eyes shut, absorbing verbal blow after blow.

Camilla poured sharp words into his ears without taking a breath. Her powdery scent invaded his nostrils from where she stood staring at him across the desk. The baby-blue dress that hugged her curves made it hard for him to concentrate. Today, she'd put her hair up, exposing her slender neck. The thought of burying his face there set a fire between his legs, and he shifted to ease his discomfort.

He massaged his nape and let his gaze settle on Dro, who was pretending to scroll through his phone while waiting so they could discuss Camilla's case.

They'd returned from an early morning meeting and Camilla had been waiting for him across from Elise's desk, cool as you please, flipping through a magazine. Fire had flashed from her eyes at the sight of him and the same heat seared him now.

Shaz knew better than to interrupt her tirade. He understood her anxieties better than she'd ever know, but he couldn't tell her. Given the mood she was in, she'd blast off his head and send it rolling from Ocho Rios all the way to Montego Bay. Her next words made him sit up straight.

"There's all this hype about you, from everybody around here." She gestured with a sweep of her hand. "Aunt Mabel seems to think the sun shines out of your ass, but it feels more like an urban myth than reality."

Dro smirked, shoulders heaving in an effort not to laugh, but kept his gaze on the screen.

"I'm not discounting what you do, really, I'm not, but I'm yet to see—"

Her words hit him in the gut. The past two days emergencies with his other clients and the business with The Castle ate up a big chunk of his time, but her predicament was partly why Dro was sitting in his office trying not to bust a gut. Shaz had put him to work and now planned to pick his brain to get more insight on how they could expedite her application for an extension on her time in the country.

Although his profession was crisis management, Dro could definitely put Shaz in touch with the right people. That's how far he was prepared to go for her, but she was hearing none of that. Shaz kept his tone even because he didn't want her to think for a minute he was at the same level of annoyance as she.

"Has it occurred to you that my other clients' affairs are just as important as yours?"

Camilla finally took a breath and blanched at his words. "I'm not saying they aren't, but—"

"And that even though we haven't seen each other in a couple of days." His gaze shot to Dro, who was still occupied with his phone but had sat up a bit straighter. "I'm trying to find an avenue to resolve your situation?"

"I don't ..." She paused, as if considering his words, then shot a pointed look at Dro, who smartly avoided the heat of her gaze.

"You obviously don't know me, but trust, if I haven't said anything it's because I have nothing to report." He let that sink in as she huffed and clamped down on her next words. "Even so, my silence doesn't mean I'm not working."

His voice must have given away his irritation because Dro cocked one eyebrow and tipped his head toward him.

Shaz angled the seat sideways to avoid his former classmate's stare and focused on the potted silver queen across the room.

"Okay, so maybe I'm being a little unfair," she confessed.

One side of his mouth tilted in a smile. "Maybe?"

Camilla let out her breath in an audible sigh. "Okay, maybe a lot."

"So, here's the situation. This is a colleague of mine." He gestured to a half-smiling Dro. "Who I'm about to brainstorm with to come up with some solutions to your problem."

She gave Dro a once-over, frowned, but said, "Sounds good. When will you have an update for me?"

Shaz spared a glance for Dro, whose unwavering gaze was now fixed on him. "I don't know ..." He made her wait for a few more seconds before adding. "Maybe by tomorrow."

"You're not nice," she protested, disturbing Shaz with that melodious lilt to her words.

With a lift of one eyebrow, Shaz said, "Well, when you treat me this way ..."

He hid a grin when Dro frowned, then raised his gaze to the ceiling.

"Camilla, let us do our jobs. We'll talk later."

She stormed from the room, throwing him a glare as she pulled the door shut. Twice in one week for her to be so angry with him was not a good sign. He closed his eyes for a second and inhaled the arousing scent he'd come to associate with Camilla.

While clearing his throat unnecessarily, Shaz tried to maintain a serious expression despite Dro's amusement.

Dro grinned, then asked, "So you call me over here to sort out your issues, and you're making love to the woman with your eyes?"

"Sorry, man." Shaz stifled a smile and forced his mind back to business. "Despite how that looks or sounds, we haven't gone *there* as yet."

Dro laid his cell on the desk and pulled the lapels of his black jacket together. "What are you waiting for?"

"Her issues are much more important than our attraction to each other. After we get her business sorted out, it'll be time enough for personal stuff."

"Agreed, so here's what I found out." Dro smoothed a hand over his hair. "The boyfriend, or should I say the ex, is aware of what's happening. Apparently, he had a hand in the proposed adoption."

"You're saying he's involved in this?"

Dro nodded. "The Bennett's lawyer had the paperwork drawn up and are ready to proceed with adopting the little girl."

Shaz slumped in the executive chair. "How do you even think about giving up the child you fathered for adoption in a situation like this?"

Dro let his gaze drift to the document on the desk, and Shaz knew he wasn't telling him everything. "Did you know they had a falling out?"

Shrugging, Shaz said, "Well, they're not together anymore, so—"

"I mean, since that." He passed a hand over his mouth. Then, he sighed. "This guy is something else. Let's just say money changed hands between him and Darryl Bennett."

Shaz jack-knifed out of the chair. "You mean he sold his daughter?"

"Basically." Dro closed his eyes, then added, "And I've found out about other irregularities with people in similar plights as Camilla."

Pacing the floor with both hands in his pockets, Shaz asked, "You're telling me we have children being taken from their parents by these rich assholes simply because they can?"

"Unfortunately."

"Is there a way we can stop them?" Shaz paused in his efforts to wear a path on the tiles, then leaned in, supporting his weight with both hands on the desk, glaring at Dro.

"You can be intimidating as hell. You know that?" Dro taunted.

"Yeah, yeah." Waving that aside, Shaz continued, "Well?"

Dro's dimples made an appearance when he smiled. "There's a way to do anything you want to do in this life. It's just a matter of making the right connections." He sat forward. "As we both know, there's a wrong way and a right way to do everything. I have a friend who's high up in social services who can put some pressure on the lawyer involved in this arrangement."

Shaz frowned and reclaimed his seat, keeping a laser focus on Dro. "Sounds good. We need to make that contact like yesterday."

"Agreed." Dro slid the cell off the desk and speed-dialed a number. After a moment, he left a message and dropped the phone in the pocket of his jacket. "No answer, but she'll get back to me. She's the real deal."

Glancing at the file on his desk, Shaz scanned the top document again. "In following through for Camilla, I did see some disturbing patterns. They seemed harmless. Maybe because I expect people associated with Khalil and The Castle to be of a certain caliber. If we're both noticing this stuff, then it's another item we have to put on the agenda for our next meeting."

"Khalil was right. They turned the place upside down in his absence," Dro said, pulling the dark slashes of his brows together. "It's like the entire place is crawling with corruption."

"Outside of the good we see being done by a few of the organizations on the property, of course."

Nodding, Dro added, "And even then, it makes you wonder if they are hiding something."

"The thing is, it's easy to get away with some things. For example, Camilla's situation is far from unique. This same thing has happened in the past and still continues today." His attention strayed to the manila folder again. "Far more frequently than I care to think about."

Dro leaned forward in his seat. "Are you saying—"

The office phone buzzed, and Shaz hit the handsfree button. "Yes, Elise."

"There's someone here to see you." She lowered her voice to a near whisper. "He doesn't have an appointment but insists on seeing you."

"Did he say what it was about?" Shaz went to the coat stand and shrugged into his jacket, which he knew made him look as formidable as his fellow King sitting across the room.

"Yes, he said it has to do with an adoption."

Shaz's gaze shot to Dro, who sat forward and raised one eyebrow.

As Shaz smoothed the gray material over his chest, he asked, "What's his name?"

"Darryl Bennett."

CHAPTER 35

"This is not about you, Dwayne," Khalil said. "It's not even about The Kings. It's about what you and the kings together can do for others." Khalil poured ice water into a Styrofoam cup on his hospital tray, then offered it to Dwayne.

Dwayne leaned forward in his chair, accepting it and taking a few sips. "But I know what I can do for others. I do it every day, and that is liberating, motivating, and activating the minds of young people so that they'll be able to make a difference in the world." He returned the half-empty cup to the tray. "Why do I have to become part of this to do something as simple as that?"

A quiet laugh escaped from Khalil's mouth. "Liberate, motivate, and activate. You're rhyming almost as much as Dr. Jesse Jackson and Dr. Seuss." His smile was replaced by a reflective glance at Dwayne, who had laughed at the older man's observations. "You always had the heart of a poet, and that's what set you apart from the others." Khalil placed a hand on Dwayne's more massive one. "I do know the importance of what you do. But humor me for just a minute, will you?"

Dwayne nodded as a nurse slid into the room.

"Everything all right in here?" she asked with a warm smile.

"Yes, thank you, Christine."

She swept out of the room after adjusting the curtains to let more sunlight in. Dwayne took in the surroundings. "If I didn't see the rails on that bed and all the equipment, I'd swear this was the Marriott."

"Trust me, the food is good here, but not that good."

"Sort of like the cafeteria food at Macro," Dwayne teased.

"Heeeeey," Khalil protested. "I chose that menu myself."

"And that's my point," he shot back, and they shared a laugh.

"The Kings of the Castle ..." Khalil mused. "Why do you think they—men who started out in life the same way as you did—call themselves Kings?"

"I don't know," Dwayne replied, standing and moving closer to the window as he reflected on the eight powerful men who had shown up at his house and filled it with their presence. His family couldn't stop talking about them and how wonderful they were in their approach for plans involving The Castle and Dwayne's part in all of it.

"I don't think it's because they want to rule over everybody else," Dwayne admitted, pressing a hand to the cool glass. "Maybe they're making a statement that every person should behave like and expect to be treated like royalty. That's not what I aspire to."

Khalid was silent so long that Dwayne didn't think he would speak again. Finally, Dwayne looked in his direction and then the conversation resumed with Khalil saying, "We boast about America being a democracy, but you'd better believe that in this day and age, our country is overflowing with men who claim they are kings." He smiled. "And I don't mean The Kings of the Castle."

Dwayne reclaimed his seat, then sat forward in his chair. "I see where you're coming from. Everyone readily identifies a king as the person who has the right to rule over a people and land. Sometimes that right is passed down through a bloodline. But often, that right comes by one man killing off another and taking his place at the top of the totem pole. That happens on the streets all the time. And it happens in politics and business. That's why it isn't for me. Like I told the others, I'm going to stay in my lane before I end up on the shoulder or in a ditch."

"Okay, so if I follow that line of thinking you had about your brothers earlier," Khalil hedged. "Tell me the most important characteristics of royalty or a king in your eyes."

Dwayne pursed his lips and looked upward before saying, "For starters, a king needs to be meek, meaning that he is strong, but he knows when to use his strength and when to harness it for the greater good."

"Agreed. Keep going."

"And he needs to be grounded." Dwayne thought about his own life, the issues that had shadowed his twin and the family secrets that had nearly destroyed them. "Life's challenges might sometimes knock him to his knees, but he won't lay there and play the victim. He'll push himself to regain focus on what he was put on this earth to accomplish, and that will propel him to keep moving forward in spite of what life throws at him."

"Well put. More?"

Dwayne scooped up the cup and polished off the rest of the water. He mulled over what he'd already said, then added, "The best kinds of kings are the ones who aren't afraid to help those under them to become the best they can be."

Khalil nodded.

"And it goes without saying that any good king protects his subjects."

Khalil nodded again, and it almost seemed as if a smile played about the corners of his lips. As though the conversation was going exactly the way he had planned. "Go on."

"Having principles and integrity is important. He needs to have a sound moral compass because he sets the tone for the kingdom. The rules and guidelines he puts in place should provide structure and order that benefits the people. He shouldn't yoke the people with regulations that only satisfy his selfish wants and needs."

Khalil laced his hands and placed them on top of the white bedsheet.

"And he ought to be a giver, not a taker. A good king is willing to bless his people."

"It was pretty easy for you to list those characteristics," Khalil whispered. "Do you know why?"

Dwayne was reluctant to give voice to his thoughts because he already knew that the conversation had streamed into the exact points that Khalil would have made without Dwayne's input.

"Because every one of those traits is a natural part of who you are." Khalil placed one of his hands over Dwayne's heart. "I can say the same about each of The Kings too. But there's one characteristic that trumps all of those. It's a person's ability to see the truth about how their own thoughts and actions help or hinder their forward progress. See, a *good* king might acknowledge some of his strengths and weaknesses. But a *great* king makes room in his inner circle for trusted experts who can advise him so that his ignorance, weaknesses, or limitations won't become a liability to his kingdom. That's what the Kings need. A wise counselor. Someone with the voice of reason. Dwayne, you are the man who fits that bill."

Dwayne stood, feeling the weight of the decision upon him. He embraced a simple life, but this appointment required so much more.

"So, the question is, are you okay with using your God-given strengths just to better *some* of our youth? Or do you want to use them to the fullest by perfecting these men who will touch the lives of more young people than you could ever touch alone?"

CHAPTER 36

"Baby boy, they don't know who they're dealing with," Brandi's voice boomed through the Jag's speaker.

"Aunt Bee…" Daron turned the knob on the dashboard to lower the Bluetooth's volume. "I have a friend looking into it who's familiar with Chicago's streets and their players."

"Good," she huffed. "Those suits you hired last time didn't know enough about hood hits to recognize a trademark."

"Just let me handle this." Daron was glad the vehicle was moving because even with the window down and the volume lowered, Brandi's tone sounded as though she was yelling through a bullhorn.

"No, I'm seeing this through."

Daron sighed his frustration. Determination was an asset until a person was on a fool's mission. He wished he had more personal time to devote to getting his aunt to accept that his brother's death was an accident. On top of everything else he had going, Daron had agreed to work with an old friend on a project.

As if he'd been summoned, the name Calvin Atwood appeared on the Jag's screen. "I have to take this call. We'll finish this conversation later."

He switched over the call before she could protest. "Did you get my notes?"

Daron rolled up the window, cutting off the warm air flowing in, knowing Calvin wouldn't be half as loud as his aunt.

"Let me tell you, I've been grateful for the help you've provided over the years on the development of the Emperor's Suit," Calvin said, referring to a spectacular invention that made the wearer of the device invisible to the naked eye. Several governments had sent teams to kill Calvin simply to make off with the project for their own purpose. Thanks to a woman a security firm paired Calvin up with, they'd been unsuccessful. Though that didn't keep them from trying. "I'm happy as hell that your schedule finally opened up. Now we can work on this final phase together."

"Why are you splitting the contract in half?"

Daron had agreed to work on incorporating a tracker and camera into The Suit before he knew that Calvin was attempting to broker a three-billion-dollar deal with a three-million-dollar payout upon signing the contract. From what Daron heard, higher bids were coming in and that kind of money was nothing to take lightly.

"You'll be an equal partner in the danger," Calvin huffed.

"Unfortunately, I'm not a stranger to risk associated with projects like this. But you know that's not the issue."

"We can battle it out over the terms another time."

"I want to talk to you about something urgent that has come up."

Daron explained about inheriting the membership and Khalil's proposal for him to team up with other men to tackle the challenges of The Castle.

"Originally, I had no intention of accepting something associated with Bishop, because I'm still trying to recover from the fallout of issues he left hanging. However, I felt a strong sense of obligation when it came to these new responsibilities, hoping it would be a benefit in sparking youth all over the United States to dream big."

"I hear you," Calvin said. "It amazes me how many low-income children haven't been exposed to people like us, especially with STEM programs on the rise."

"Not only that, but I also want to help convince a woman, who already has a plan to help those in need, that the time is now to step into her purpose. At the end of the day, before I even knew about the membership, I was hired for a job to protect someone within The Castle walls."

Daron briefly spoke about the security contract he had with The Castle and requested to use The Suit. "People have already tried to kill Khalil and his son. I'd like to make sure he can move about undetected."

"That explains two Suits, assuming one is for you, but you asked for eleven."

"I'd like to protect the other eight men representing him. The additional one is for the expert I may need to call in."

Daron told him a little about the Castle's premise—the public parts—causing Calvin to give a low whistle of approval. "Wow, that's pretty huge. I'll see what I can do. Any chance that I …"

"It has to be nine men," Daron said, anticipating the question. "I'll put in a word for you since one of the men isn't interested in claiming his seat at the table."

Daron wrapped up the call as he maneuvered through the light street traffic heading to drop off his house keys to Cameron before another meeting at The Castle. This time, a more formal undertaking.

He parked, noticing a Bentley Flying Spur he'd never seen before on the street alongside the Community Center.

Daron stepped out, making sure his weapon was in easy reach. The tinted windows didn't allow him to see whether anyone was inside. A few vehicles passed on the main road but there wasn't much activity on the streets. The warm breeze blew the debris at his feet, but another sound caught his attention before he heard, "You're a hard man to find."

Just steps away from the Community Center, Daron turned toward the nasally voice and found a slim, short man with wide blue eyes, thin lips, and sunburnt skin who had an intense glare. Marquise Sinclair, leader of an art theft ring. According to the file his assistant had given him, Marquise became a member of The Castle for the power and the network to back up his schemes.

"Why are you even looking?" Daron noticed the muscular man who had been the group leader at the date night incident in the garage, leaning on a gray Bentley.

Marquise gave a stilted smile. "Just want to make an offer."

"You have nothing I want."

"I have the power to make sure that three-million-dollar deal you're working on with Dr. Atwood doesn't disappear."

Daron chuckled, knowing Marquise's contact was high enough up to have some of the facts, but not all, if he knew exactly how much was involved, they would be having an entirely different conversation. "That sounds more like a threat than an offer."

"It's the same thing." Marquise glanced up at the darkening sky, taking in the clouds gathering in a sure sign of an upcoming rainstorm, then returned his focus to Daron. "It's a question of do you want to do things the easy way or the hard way?"

Daron pressed the device in the pocket of his jacket to prevent the Community Center's security cameras from recording. "How does having me accept this offer benefit you?" His opposite hand rested next to a Beretta holstered on his waist, a move that didn't go unnoticed by Marquise's backup.

"Bishop should have given me his seat. You're not even remotely interested in what's going on in that place right now. All you need to do is not allow The Castle to transfer into the hands of these new men when it's time to decide its future."

"And if I don't?"

"Considering you inherited the membership from Bishop, you know the deal." Marquise looked over his shoulder, and the muscle-bound man advanced across the street until he stood by his side. "Don't let Khalil and Vikkas get you twisted and have your life lying in ruins."

"Bishop and I have several things in common." Daron stepped forward, unbothered by the attempt to intimidate him. "We make our own decisions and are not easily influenced by others. *And* we don't take kindly to threats."

"I hear you have a beautiful lady friend," Marquise snarled, inching closer as the bodyguard pulled out a weapon of his own. "I'd hate for her to pay the cost of your unfortunate decision."

Before the muscular man could react, Daron wrapped a hand around Marquise's neck then whipped out the Beretta, aiming at the tough guy's head. "And I hear you have a death wish."

"We're only here to make a business proposition." Marquise struggled to remove Daron's hand but to no avail.

"Sounded more like you were trying to make an enemy than an ally." He tightened the grip on the man's neck before releasing his hold. The weapon stayed trained on his goon.

Marquise cracked his neck, then glanced over his shoulder before wriggling his fingers. The goon produced a small black and gold envelope, which Marquise grabbed and tried to pass to Daron. "I'm going to give you some time and incentive to accept the offer."

Marquise tossed the envelope on Daron's car.

"What's that?" Daron's gaze never left the two of them as Marquise begin inching away, gesturing for the other man to follow.

When they made it to the Bentley, Marquise glanced back at Daron. "It's the time and place I'm going to need that answer. Enjoy the taste of what will happen if you choose wrong."

Before Daron could respond, Marquise had slipped into the back seat and closed the door. Daron crushed the envelope as the Bentley pulled away. He looked back to see Cameron's face in the window. She turned away, but he could have sworn her expression had turned dark.

CHAPTER 37

Reno's focus was keener than a sharp-shooter stalking its prey as he eyed the man responsible for the increased gang and drug activity near the transitional apartment grounds, a place where they housed women who came to them under the most extreme circumstances. The man had disposable wealth, so Reno couldn't understand why he chose to live his life that way.

Frank Maddox, who leaned against the brick wall under the *smoking prohibited* sign, puffed a Black & Mild outside of the café where they agreed to meet. Reno quickly zeroed in on the firearm tucked in the waistband of his pants. The weapon wasn't even concealed, which meant that Frank was as crazy as he was brazen. Only law enforcement paraded their guns around as such. Reno heeded the overt warning and opted for an introduction as Khalil's former student and mentee.

The outdoor eating area was filled with patrons and their families, sitting under a brass awning with beautiful pastel flowers hanging above. A sweet cinnamon aroma swirled in the air as the servers traveled in and out of the café doors with dessert orders on trays. Reno envisioned him and Zuri partaking in afternoon delights at this place. The corners of his lips upturned, that is, until he shook the tender sentiment and focused on the only thing daunting about the atmosphere—the man who obviously didn't belong.

"Good Morning," Reno greeted, extending his hand to Frank, taking in his grandiose stature and wondered what he had done to become so huge. Steroids were the first things that came to mind.

Frank blew a smoke ring in the air, dropped the butt, then stomped it with his foot. "I know who you are, Mariano DeLuca, son of Giacomo and Emma DeLuca. Tell Vicente and Sofia I said hello."

His parent's names were common knowledge, but when Frank rattled off the names of his brother and sister, he'd be lying if he said that didn't surprise him more than a little. But Frank wasn't the only one who did his homework.

"Most certainly," Reno responded, lowering his hand. "Be sure to give your wife, Tina, and your lovely daughter, Ava, my regards as well."

For Frank to be a larger than life drug lord, his poker face needed much work. He narrowed the space between them and muttered, "Do you know who you're playing with?" Frank's right hand disappeared behind his back.

From his peripheral, Reno caught a glimpse of Kaleb rising from a table off to the side. He knew better than to trust a gangster, and although he couldn't point anyone out specifically, Reno knew Frank wasn't alone. So, he also had backup just in case things got out of hand. Reno wouldn't let it get that far; too many innocent people were present, especially women and children.

Disregarding the question without breaking eye contact, Reno said, "Have a seat," as he pulled out a chair, unbuttoned his blazer, and lowered into the basket-weave cushioned patio chair.

Frank remained standing. His knitted brows and cold stare said he wasn't ready to let the exchange go. Reno was aware he'd turned the tables on the seasoned criminal. More than anything, Reno would bet his life that Frank wasn't accustomed to anyone administering open threats to his face.

"I'm considering an opportunity and I would like your input," Reno said, leaning back into the chair, hoping to disarm the brute of his anger. "From what I hear, you've been a Castle member for quite some time.

Anything you can share would be appreciated in helping me make an informed decision."

Frank's knitted brows didn't move an inch. "Watch yourself, DeLuca," he warned, pointing his index finger at Reno, then tilting his head, closing one eye, and bending his thumb as if shooting Reno between the eyes. "No one threatens my family and lives to see another day."

He stalked off and two other men sitting among the patrons followed behind him to an awaiting SUV with black-tinted windows. Frank and Reno exchanged eye contact right before Frank stepped into the vehicle and peeled away.

"That didn't go as planned," Kaleb said, claiming the seat across from Reno.

"Definitely not, but now I'm sure more than ever that I should to accept my appointment at The Castle," Reno said with certainty, leaning forward. "First, as a way to pay homage to Khalil for all that he's done for me—for us. Second, for the unlimited resources." Reno paused, rubbing his hands together.

"What's your little mastermind cooking up over there?" Kaleb asked, giving Reno the side-eye. "Does it have anything to do with Zuri?"

Reno chuckled. "Yes, but not the way you're thinking."

"I'm listening," Kaleb said, flagging down the waitress.

"It's about keeping Zuri and all of the women safe, then maybe we—"

"I knew you were into her," Kaleb shot back, pounding his fist lightly on the table.

Shaking his head, Reno grinned. "I'll admit, she does it for me, but first things first. We're going to meet with the rest of our brothers and formulate a plan to exterminate the thorn threatening the women's safety."

"Frank Maddox?" Kaleb asked, glancing to the spot the SUV had vacated.

"Most definitely."

CHAPTER 38

Dro tipped one brow and flashed Shaz a grin. "If you'd stop looking at your watch, maybe we could get some things done."

The restaurant Shaz chose for their meeting was a popular one and had a fair number of people inside, so Shaz also kept an eye on the entrance. He didn't want to miss Camilla when she arrived. "Very funny. I only looked once and that was because—"

With both hands in the air, Dro stopped him. "Yeah, yeah. We both know you can't wait to see Camilla."

Shaz bit back a chuckle. "That might be true, but it has nothing to do with anything happening at this table."

"In that case, why'd you look over my shoulder just now?"

With one hand on a bottle of Red Stripe Light Sorrel Beer, Shaz scoffed. "Whatever, man. Anyway, to get back to what you were saying …"

"Finally." Dro leaned toward Shaz as he took a swig of beer. "That King member—Darryl Bennett—is in deeper than I thought at first. Aside from trying to get his hands on Camilla's baby, seems he has a major hand in these rigged adoptions that lead into some of the children ending up as unwilling organ donors."

A flash of anger filled him. Camilla's child could not end up that way. No child should. Stroking his locks, Shaz frowned at the beer bottle then asked, "That would mean he has more connections than we know."

"Bennett coming to see you was an attempt to fool you into thinking—"

"He was a victim of circumstances, or something."

"Or something, is right." Dro took a sip from his club soda and lime. "I'm not one-hundred percent sure yet, but I think he's some sort of broker in this business which is also tied to the immigrant children the current administration is snatching from the parents and putting into detention camps."

Shaz studied his hands, which lay on the table. The news kept getting worse with every word. "I'm sure he'll learn I wasn't born this big, as my mother likes to say. I've got some experience to back things up."

"Won't he be in for a surprise," Dro agreed, before they both burst out laughing.

After their laughter trickled away, Dro spun the glass on the table as he scanned the room.

"So, what have you decided regarding taking up Khalil's offer on The Castle business?" he asked Dro.

Dro's voice faded a little, while Shaz sat up and threw a glance toward the doorway of the restaurant. He resisted the desire to check the time. He'd scheduled his meeting with Dro for a half hour before his lunch date with Camilla. Fifteen minutes had gone by since they'd been seated, and he'd prefer if Dro was out of the picture when she turned up. Dro would give him hell if Camilla dragged him over the coals like last time.

"Earth to Shaz. Earth to Shaz."

When he looked at Dro, the man had one hand fisted over his mouth, forming a loudspeaker, while his eyes danced in a private laugh at Shaz's expense.

Shaz sucked his teeth. "I'm very much here." He let his gaze settle on the bar situated on the other side of the room before connecting with Dro again. "I have to tell you, the main reason I'd be interested in any of this is because of what happened to Khalil and the debt I owe him, and ..." Again, his attention drifted to the doorway. "Camilla. The Castle would extend my reach, give me more access to people who could influence her situation. She's got me ..."

"Twisted up seven ways to Sunday?"

Throwing Dro a glare, Shaz said, "You're certainly on a roll. When the tables turn, I'll remember how you treated me."

He swallowed more of the red-tinted beer. "So, like I was saying, what's going on in that place hit me right here." Shaz patted his abs. "I admit my history has a lot to do with what I'm feeling and if I can help anybody else avoid being torn from their family or used as pawns in the way that Bennett sets things up, that's what I'm gonna do. What about you?"

With a slow nod, Dro said. "I think I'm on board. It means juggling my schedule to fulfill my role, but it's doable. Membership has its privileges."

A slow smile spread over Shaz's face and he folded his arms over his chest. "I like the sound of that. You're a fixer by nature, so turning things around is right up your alley."

Once more, his focus strayed to the doorway, where Camilla now stood. A tiny frown pulled her brows together as she scanned the restaurant. When she spotted him, Camilla's expression shifted, and a smile lit her face. She wore another of those ankle-length numbers that skimmed her curves and made him wonder what was underneath.

His heart rate accelerated, but Shaz kept his smile from turning into a goofy grin. Looking back at Dro, he tipped his head toward Camilla. "Hit the road. Camilla just walked in."

"Is this how you treat your friends?" Dro said as he got to his feet.

When Shaz rose, they shook hands and exchanged a man hug. By the time they stood apart, Camilla had arrived at the table with a hostess guiding her. Shaz asked the hazel-eyed woman to send them a waitress in a minute then he helped Camilla into her seat.

Meanwhile, Dro was acting the part of host. "Hey, Camilla. Everything good?"

"Yes, thanks," she said, with a bright smile.

Shaz peered at her, thinking she was expert at hiding her emotions. Having spent some time with her, he was more attuned to her moods.

The anxiety she carried with her hadn't disappeared. She simply cloaked it when necessary.

"It's good seeing you again," Dro said and left them with a charming smile that made Shaz want to pop him one.

"Nice guy," Camilla said, as Shaz sat. "I forgot to thank him for the help he's given me so far."

"Not to worry, I'll convey your thanks." Shaz was surprised at the sour note in his voice and hoped Camilla hadn't caught it. The woman had him acting out of character. Dro had his own love interest, so Shaz had no need to be jealous. And yet, Camilla stirred emotions inside him that he hadn't experienced in a long time.

As their gazes met, he gauged that for all outward purposes Camilla seemed fine, but he'd tread carefully and find out how she was really doing in a bit. "Would you like to order?" he asked.

Shaking her head, she hid a grin. "I'm sorry, but I've already eaten. I stopped by Aunt Mabel's before I got here. She forced some stewed peas on me."

Shaz assumed a sober expression and laid a hand on his stomach. "And she didn't send me any? Tell her I'm wounded."

Camilla rolled her eyes. "Did you expect me to walk in here carrying a food carton from another restaurant?"

He tapped her hand and injected a teasing note into his voice, "Where there's a will, there's a way. Next time, bring me some of dat mmm-mmm goodness. Did it have pig's tail?"

Laughing, Camilla said, "You know it did. And salt beef. And spinners. She said you like those little dumplings."

"She's right, and you're a cruel woman for even bringing that up." Shaz licked his lips and acted as if his eyes rolled back into his head on their own, which made Camilla chuckle.

"I'm sorry. Yeah, I'm a terrible tease." She turned her hand over and squeezed his. "I'll make it up to you."

As warmth spread in his belly and shot southward, Shaz linked their fingers together. "Promise?"

Camilla tried to withdraw her hand, but Shaz wouldn't let her. "Don't," he said softly.

Her eyes went to their joined hands on top of the table and turned cloudy. A mixture of guilt and sadness crept over her features, and he wanted to comfort her. At a guess, he'd say she felt bad for exchanging jokes with him when her issues with her baby were still unresolved.

"What d'you mean?" She slid her hand from his.

"It's okay to have this interlude with me," he whispered. "Nothing in life says we can't have good moments even when our situation seems as black as midnight."

A grimace crossed her face. "Easy for you to say. You're not in my position."

"We both know I'm doing the best I can for you and Ayanna."

After a moment, Camilla sighed and raised her head. "Yeah. You are. It's just that sometimes I get impatient, especially with the time going by at the speed of a horse running down a track on race day."

"I get that. But I'm here for you. You know that."

If they weren't sitting in full view of a bunch of people, he'd have pulled her to him and sampled her lips the way he had when they kissed that first time. He was sure she read his thoughts because her eyes went dark and she turned her head away as if to avoid interfacing with him.

Camilla was definitely into him. He wished she'd relax and go with the flow, even if right now they could only go so far based on her status as his client.

She licked her lips and mussed her hair by running one hand through it. "I know you are." Her voice dropped to a whisper. "And I appreciate you more than I can say."

He wanted more than that from her, and he clasped her hand again as a man loomed over the table. Shaz tipped his head back but didn't let his expression change when he recognized Darryl Bennett.

"Didn't expect to see you here," the strapping older man said while his focus shifted to Camilla. "But I'm glad we ran into each other."

"I wonder why." Shaz got to his feet. "I believe we said all we had to say at my office."

"I doubt that," Bennett said, holding out one hand.

Shaz hesitated but shook it after a few seconds. Bennett's grip was firm to the point of being painful, but Shaz refused to wince or crush the man's hand in return. The ploy was childish at best and twisted at worst. Typical of a corrupt politician. Even in a handshake, the man was trying to strong-arm Shaz.

As Bennett loosened his grip, a tic danced around his eye. "I still need to talk with you. I have an offer I'm sure you won't be able to refuse, especially since ..." He dropped his pitch. "I hear you will be taking a seat on the board of directors at The Castle."

Hands on both sides of his waist, Shaz raised both eyebrows and decided to keep his business to himself. "I'm not sure where you heard that, but I haven't made a decision."

"The Castle's business can be demanding ... and dangerous," Bennett warned. "You may want to think carefully before you decide whether to accept the position."

If he'd had a doubt about going all-in, this man's veiled threat made up his mind for him. Shaz's gaze was steady when he said. "Thank you for that advice. Unsolicited, though it may be."

Heat flared in Bennett's eyes, and Shaz suppressed the smirk rising to the surface. The older man straightened, smoothed the lapels of his jacket and stepped back. His gaze flicked to Camilla and came back to Shaz. "You're welcome, and as far as I'm concerned, we still have business to discuss."

Shaz let his smile come through but kept his tone terse. "Let's agree to disagree."

Bennett spun on his heels and walked away.

Shaz took his seat, acknowledging the anger in Camilla's eyes. "No worries. This business is being handled," he said. "Now, where were we?"

CHAPTER 39

"Fellas, I have to make a run," Vikkas said, checking his screen and frowning.

The men paused in their conversations aimed at fleshing out what their roles would be in The Castle.

"Looks like there's a little bit of trouble at Milan's office."

"What kind of trouble?" Daron asked, piping up from his chair at the boardroom table.

"The kind that's going to take about fifty grand and my presence to resolve."

"Your woman is asking for that kind of money straight out the gate?" Kaleb asked, his eyes widening to the size of dinner plates. "I ain't saying she's a gold—"

"No," he snapped, still scanning the screen. "Her assistant has her phone. She's hiding out in the office and just texted that Seth—Milan's brother—showed up to the office with some big dudes. They're not letting anyone leave until that money walks in."

"Let's ride fellas," Daron said, peering over Vikkas' shoulder to read the message for himself.

"And do what? They're asking for fifty grand within the hour," Shaz said, coming to stand near Vikkas and Daron. "You have fifty grand just laying around?"

"Actually …" Daron grinned and checked his watch. "We'll just need to make a stop on the way there. I'll explain the plan before we get to the center."

* * *

"See, here's what we're not going to do," Vikkas said an hour later, as the two men posted at the entrance of the center frisked him for non-existent weapons. "You're not going to hold my woman hostage over some bullshit. She's worth every penny you're asking, but I'm not giving you one dime."

The employees had all been rounded up from their cubicles and stood under guard against the back wall of the office. Toni was not present and accounted for.

A pale, stocky man waved his gun before pointing it at Milan. "She'll still be worth it if I bust a cap in her ass?"

"She most definitely will," Vikkas shot back. "But you won't. Trust me on that."

Milan frowned and focused on the window as several shadows flickered past. Then her gaze lowered to the row of plastic chairs across from the reception desk as though trying to figure something out. Everywhere else, but where he wanted her to focus. Vikkas flinched and tried to get her attention. When she finally locked a gaze with him, he gave her a look which translated to, *knock it off.*

A head appeared over a far section of the drywall as Toni peeped over one of the cubicles. At the sight of the guns, she disappeared as fast as she'd appeared. Apparently, they missed her on their first pass.

"I mean, ain't you guys supposed to pay her family something?" another one of the criminals said, plopping down on Toni's desk and causing her porcelain angel to slide onto the ground.

"Bride price," Vikkas answered. "Yes, but that is negotiated with her father."

Milan's brother shrugged. "Well, he ain't here. He's locked up."

"Then seems like you're shit out of luck today," Vikkas shot back. "So, set it up and let's roll. Get that whole price of the bride thing together."

"Nah man, we gon' need that cash right about now," the stocky one said, tapping his gun on the desk.

Vikkas timed the last few taps, reached out and in a blink, the man's gun was in his hand, pointed at the pale guy with the hoodie.

The man didn't flinch, but his skin turned an ugly shade of crimson. "Why you pointing it at me? I ain't asking for nothing."

"Yes, but you're the one calling the shots so . . ." Vikkas shrugged.

"Put the guns down," Seth said. "We just gonna have a man to man talk, that's all."

Vikkas swept a gaze across all of the criminals in the place and asked, "Which one of you is a man?"

"Oh, you got jokes," the leader said.

"I'm just saying, it takes someone with balls to step to someone with a basic amount of common sense." Vikkas moved a little closer so the men's focus would stay on him. "So, like I said, which man? I would respect that much more than this madness you're trying to pull."

"Worked, didn't it?" the leader said with a smirk. "You're here. Outnumbered and outgunned."

"Fifty grand, right?" Vikkas queried.

"Yeah," the hoodie guy said. "That'll square thangs up."

"Bring it in," Vikkas said into his phone.

"Damn you got it like that?" Seth asked, taking his feet off the desk. "Maybe we should've asked for more."

"Yeah, that sounds good to me," the bruiser of a guy near the front door chimed in.

A few minutes later a knock on the door caused the two goons to crack it a little. Daron was on the other side.

"Is that him?" Seth asked.

Vikkas nodded and Daron was frisked before they allowed him to walk to a spot that wasn't far from Toni's desk. "Somebody call for a courier?"

"Damn, that was fast," Seth said, gesturing for Daron to come closer.

"No, bring that over here," the leader said, overriding Seth's direction and causing him to glare so hard Vikkas thought the place would catch fire. "Let's see what I got."

"What you got is a problem," Reno said, exploding into the foyer from the back exit. Grant, Kaleb, and Shaz were right behind him. They spread out and each of them had a weapon of their own, pointed at the key players. Reno tossed one each to Vikkas and Daron, who immediately positioned themselves to handle the men perched near the door, and the few at Toni's desk.

Daron, you're my mofo.

"Awww, so you brought in reinforcements," the leader taunted.

Vikkas shrugged and smiled. "You know, even things up a little. Toni, go with them."

She popped up from her hiding place, still holding Milan's phone. "Any of these brothers sing—"

"Toni!"

She scrambled away, then sprinted toward Kaleb and Grant. "I'm moving. I'm moving."

Daron lifted a duffle bag and dropped it on the ground in front of Seth and the leader. "Fifty grand, just as you requested."

Milan snapped, "Now, I'd like for all of you to get the hell up out of my—"

"If it was that easy to get this," Seth said, grinning as his buddy unzipped the bag. "Then he can get more. A lot more. Then we'd re-up supplies that'll last us the rest of the year. We'd make two million before—"

A gunshot rang out.

CHAPTER 40

Seth found himself on the wrong end of a Saturday Night Special.

He dropped to the ground, screaming as he held onto both of his knees. The pain must have been so bad that he didn't know which one was hit.

"Greedy, just plain greedy," Milan said, keeping a steady grip on her gun as the other men of Seth's crew inched back. "The man brought what you asked for, and you still aren't satisfied. Just like the rest of your family."

"My family?" he shot back, writhing on the ground. "They're your family too."

Milan rounded the reception area, moving past a low table loaded with magazines. "You all haven't been anything to me since Mama showed me the door. So don't be claiming I'm family now. Take the money and get the hell out." Toni signaled to her, then pointed vigorously at Tamika before she flashed a glare that way. "And take her with you."

"What did I do?" Tamika shrieked, clutching her fake pearls.

"You're the one who tipped my brother off to what was going on with me," Milan said, causing Dani to move away from her office and close the distance between them.

"And what did you have to gain by doing that?" Milan snapped.

"He's my man," Tamika sobbed into her hands. "I was just telling him he needed to be a lot more like Vikkas in the way he came all up in here for you. When he asked for your name, I didn't think anything of it. When I said Milan, he just smiled. Then he said we could make us some quick money. I didn't know he was going to do this." She looked at Milan. "I'm so sorry."

"About what?" Milan snapped. "That you put everyone in jeopardy to line your pockets? Really?" She poked an index finger in Tamika's chest. "Exactly what do you think would've happened with this many witnesses? Just let us go our merry little way?"

Several people in the office gasped. Dani lost every ounce of coloring. Tamika nearly turned green and stumbled backward under the realization she could have gotten everyone killed.

"You might want to split the money up before you leave," Shaz suggested, causing Vikkas and Milan to look in his direction, wondering why he would have them stall in order to do that.

Seth crawled forward, reached into the bag, pulled out a handful of bills, but couldn't manage much more. One of the men near the door came forward, tossed a stack to each of the men, though the leader looked ready to protest. Tamika held her hand out and Seth looked at it as if to say *I wish I would*. She crumbled under the weight of his disdain.

"Wait," Milan said, and the men froze. "How much is thirty pieces of silver worth these days."

"About six hundred dollars, give or take," Daron offered.

"Seth, break her off at least that much."

Grumbling, he did, practically whimpering with pain, then signaled to the rest of his crew that it was time to exit. Two of them lifted him and had to carry him out the door. The others kept their weapons drawn until every last one of their crew and Tamika had cleared the building.

Kaleb spoke into his watch. "You handled that?"

"Indeed," Jai replied.

"They're all over them," Dro chimed in.

Sirens blared, and within seconds the employees rushed toward the windows and watched as Seth and the rest of the men were blocked in and rounded up.

Milan placed a hand on her hip. "They didn't even know what they did here, so how are they—"

"I may have tipped them off to the fact that there was some counterfeit money involved," Jai said, slipping the rest of the way through the door before he came to stand next to Reno and Grant.

"Counterfeit?" Milan screeched. "You paid for me in Monopoly money? I should put a bullet in you just on—"

"No, we set them up with counterfeit money," Daron explained. "Knowing it's at least a fifteen-year prison sentence for each one of them."

"And don't forget the fine," Dro chimed in. "One that they probably won't be able to pay."

"All this without anyone getting shot," Shaz said with a smile.

"Well, about that," Vikkas said with a pointed glare at Milan. "Gunslinger here put a bullet in her brother."

"Damn," Shaz said, giving Milan a nod of respect.

Milan folded her arms across her full breasts. "Payback. He put me in a broken fridge when I was ten and left me there until I damn near died. He had it coming."

"Remind me not to get on your bad side," Vikkas said, kissing her temple.

"You *are* on my bad side. Monopoly money, really?"

"Wheeeeew, look at the time," Grant said, causing the others to laugh.

Daron held his hand out for Milan's weapon. "We need to make sure your woman gets a little more target practice. She was aiming for the nuts and hit his knees."

"Hey," Vikkas protested. "She knows how to shoot. We all had weapons and martial arts training at Macro."

"Never understood that for him to be such a peaceful man," Shaz said, placing his locs over his shoulder.

Jai chuckled. "He said peace was the preferred choice, whipping ass was always on deck if warranted."

"Someone's going to give her up for that gunshot. Do you have a conceal and carry permit?" Dro asked.

"Of course."

"She'll be out of processing in no time," Shaz said.

"I'll bring bail money," Daron said.

"No!" Vikkas and several of the brothers chorused. "We'll use plastic for this one."

"Oh, come on, fellas," Daron shot back. "It's not like I don't have the real stuff stashed away."

"Dani, I'll make sure that wall gets repaired," Vikkas said, shaking his head as the men chuckled at Daron's assertion.

Dani nodded, but her gaze was firmly planted on the other men who were with him. So were the eyes of the rest of the women in the place. Toni was damn near hyperventilating with all the testosterone close by.

"And you all need more security here," Daron said, leaning against the wall of Dani's office. "It was so easy to get through the back. And these guys waltzed in here without—"

"It's not in the budget," she said.

Dro dropped down in the reception chair and swiveled to face her. "It is now. This place needs to be secured and you need guards to keep folks from just walking up in here all willy-nilly."

"So, Vik," Toni purred, moseying up to a panic-stricken Shaz and rolling one of his locs between her fingers. "Which one of your brothers is single?"

"Careful fellas," Vikkas warned. "She wears two pairs of drawers. Must be some powerful—"

"You don't even want to know," Milan said, nudging Vikkas into silence.

The brothers gave each other curious glances before Toni huffed and stormed to her desk.

CHAPTER 41

KHALIL GERMAINE

The overstuffed couch and potted houseplant in one corner of the private room were designed to make patients forget they were in the hospital. Pity Varsha Germaine insisted on disturbing his peace.

"If you do not have Vikkas consent to marry one of the Gupta sisters," Varsha said to Khalil. "I no longer want to be your wife."

"Somehow that's not the threat you expect it to be," Khalil said, adjusting himself on the hospital bed. "And I will humbly accept your offer of divorce."

Her eyes widened to the size of saucers. "Wait, I did not—"

"You did mean it and so did I," he said, smiling because the freedom he felt in this moment was profound. Khalil's gaze traveled to the shaded window. When he focused on Varsha, his smile disappeared. "You will be well cared for. But I release you and myself from the bondage this marriage has been for both of us. I wish you a good life."

Varsha gripped the bed's silver railing. "The family will strip you of everything. Even your beloved Castle."

"Ah, the claws come out again," he whispered. "I have never wanted for any good thing and The Castle is now in the hands of its rightful owners; people who will see to its progression. There is nothing my family or your family is able to do." He inhaled and let it out slowly. "And since you were the one to issue the divorce request, I am clear of conscience and obligation."

"You can't prove I said anything of the kind," she huffed, lifting her chin in that haughty manner he had always disliked.

"Oh, but I can," he said, pressing a button on a newly implanted device his security director had given him. "Daron, would you be so kind as to play that back for my wife?"

She gasped as her words came through loud and clear over the speaker. She recovered, a smirk on her lips as she said, "Then it will also show that I recanted."

"Will it?"

Realization dawned on Varsha, and her hand flew to her bosom. "You cannot do this. I—I—I will lose favor, status—and …"

"Did you think about any of those issues when you decided to threaten me because I will not force my son into an unhappy marriage?"

Varsha lowered her gaze to the industrial tiles.

Khalil placed a hand over her trembling one. "You might want to take this lesson from the wise words of the Godfather himself. "Don't start none, won't be none. James Brown, After Divinity 1988."

Daron's laughter echoed as Varsha stormed from the room.

CHAPTER 42

Two days had passed since the guests had graced their door. Dwayne would not entertain any conversation from anyone affiliated with The Castle, the Kings, or anything. Let his sister Val tell it, he was being a royal pain in the ass.

"Ladies, me and Dwayne will clean up since you did most of the cooking tonight," Uncle Bubba said, causing Hunter to glance in his direction. "Hunter, you go with 'em. Me and my guy right here need to have a Come to Jesus meeting."

"That works for me," Val said, hooking an arm under her soon to be sister-in-law's arm. "Come on, Tiffany. Let's relax on the balcony." Hunter was right on their tails.

Dwayne gathered up the dishes and took them to the dishwasher. Uncle Bubba brought in the leftovers and began placing them in the refrigerator. While the dishwasher hummed quietly, Dwayne looked at his uncle and said, "I promised God and three white men I wouldn't join up with the Kings of the Castle."

Uncle Bubba gave a little grunt at Dwayne throwing his familiar words back at him. "Why? The TV and movies make it seem like all black men do is kill or get killed. But the Kings prove every day that Black and Brown men have value to themselves and to the world."

Dwayne wet the dishtowel, soaped it up, then began wiping down the stove. "I'm glad the Kings do that, but what does that have to do with me? I'm nothing like them. Every single one of them has some measure of wealth. I'm not into all of that. I just want my students to thrive. I want to shape the minds of our youth. That's my idea of success."

"But wasn't it you who said climbin' the ladder of success sometimes feels like tryin' to walk up a down escalator?" Uncle Bubba put away a box of aluminum foil he'd taken out of the drawer. "What you're strivin' to do for those boys is a good thing. But the young folk ain't the only ones needin' help."

"The Castle doesn't need me for sure," Dwayne countered, pausing mid-stroke. "I mean, just think about it. They have got programs for every part of the city except the west side. We're not good enough for them or something? We don't live up to their standards?"

Uncle Bubba let out a long weary sigh. "I don't think that's it at all. I think they want to have a presence in every part of Chicago. And that's where you come in."

Dwayne averted his gaze. "Yes, but if that's the case, they probably just want to exploit my students to bring notoriety to themselves. Not happening. The kids I help are too important to be treated like characters written in and out of a play just to make the leading man look good."

Leaning back against the wall, Uncle Bubba listened silently, but his expression was forbidding, as though he had become tired of the excuses.

"I get the impression that the Kings are just another "good ol' boys" club that runs on the 'it's not what you know, it's who you know" philosophy,' Dwayne admitted. "But having that mindset can cripple a person because the reality is that *who* you know might get you in the door, but it's *what* you know that will keep you from getting tossed out that same door. At least, that's the way it should be."

Uncle Bubba straightened up. "I know you better than that, Dwayne. You research everything, especially if someone asks you to be a part of somethin'. So I know you know that's not how the Kings roll. Every one of them were humble, didn't turn their nose up at nothing. A couple of them are a little dark around the edges, but what I want to know is ... what's really stoppin' you from helpin' them?"

Dwayne rubbed the back of his neck. "I'm just an educator. Not some high-profile attorney, or world-renowned businessman, or even a famous athlete. Just an educator."

"I 'spect they knew that when they asked you to join them."

"So what good could I be to them?" he probed. "My strength is in helping boys become men."

"Yeah, but sometimes good men need help becoming better men."

Dwayne placed the dish he held into the sink. "What do you mean?"

"Well, some folks give up everything in life while they chase after their goals," Uncle Bubba said, taking a seat at the table. "Even one or two of the Kings might have gone after fame and fortune at the expense of love. But look at you. You're a successful college professor now. You reach even more lives by teachin' English as a second language at night. Your charter school is almost open, despite all the hurdles placed in front of you." He smiled. "And I know it's going to be a success. And all along the way, you managed to keep the love of a good woman and the love of your family." He gestured to the extra chairs in the living room that had been placed at the table to accommodate their hungry guests two days ago. "I'd bet at least a couple of the Kings wish they could say that. They could learn just as much from you as you can from them."

Dwayne left the sink and dropped down into the nearest seat.

"And what I like most is that they didn't laugh or correct me every time I mentioned Google."

"I was surprised at that, Unc, considering that you kept saying 'giggle' instead of Google," Dwayne protested.

"Yeah, but they knew what I meant," he said, grinning. "All I'm sayin' is that even Kings need someone to polish their crowns." Uncle Bubba gave an affirming nod. "It's time to stop hidin' your light under a bushel and step into your greatness."

CHAPTER 43

Dro sped through the gate of his parents' family home in San Miguel de Allende. His hands gripped the steering wheel, flexing and relaxing intermittently. Being summoned by his father and having to travel back to Mexico hadn't been factored into his schedule for the week. Not that he'd ever say no. Victor Reyes wasn't a man anyone said 'no' to, especially family. He'd tested the waters to see if he could re-schedule for the following week when work wasn't so hectic and The Castle business had been concluded, but his mother had shot that down.

"Alejandro, you know your father wouldn't have called you home if it wasn't important," she'd said in fluent Spanish.

He knew it, but he'd tried anyway.

Pulling his rental in front of the six-car garage, Dro hopped out and grabbed an overnight bag from the back seat. Striding across the driveway, he took the stone front steps two at a time. His hand hadn't reached the doorknob before it opened.

Their housekeeper's ample body almost took up the entire space. Laura's face relayed excitement at his arrival. Before Dro could escape, she yanked him into her firm embrace. His face was plastered against her bosom.

"Welcome home," she cried, and her enthusiasm was contagious.

"Thanks," he murmured with the little air he possessed.

She released him before stepping aside. "I've got your favorite chilies ready."

He took a deep breath before picking up the bag he'd dropped at her embrace. "Thanks, Laura. Can you let my mother know I'm going to settle in, then I'll be in to see Dad."

"Why don't you tell her yourself?" said a warm voice behind him.

Dro turned to see his mother walking towards him. Setting his case on the steps, he rushed to greet her.

"Hola, Mamá."

Valentina hugged her son before stepping back to look at him.

"You're too skinny. Why haven't you been eating?"

"I'm just fine," he dismissed.

His luggage forgotten, they walked arm in arm down the hallway and out the door into the inner courtyard.

The Reyes Mansion was a seven-bedroom, seven-bath Spanish colonial mansion. All of the rooms at the back of the house led out onto the massive patio that surrounded a large pool deck complete with seating, outdoor dining, and gardens. His father was stretched out on a chaise lounge reading a newspaper. He set it aside when he heard them coming.

Not one for raising his voice, Victor waited until his wife and son were within earshot before he greeted them. "How was the flight?"

"It was fine, Papa. Uneventful." Dro perched on the end of the lounger and faced his father. "But you didn't ask me here for small talk, did you?"

Smiling, Victor took a sip of his iced tea. "I never tire of your company, but no, I didn't."

"Has there been a change in your condition?"

"No," Valentina soothed before shooting a glance at her husband. "But he still has to take it easy."

Dro relaxed.

"How's Khalil?" Victor slid off a pair of sunglasses. "Is he still in the hospital?"

"Yes, they're still waiting to see if there's permanent damage. I've seen him. All of the guys have."

"Did he ask you to take over my position?"

Dro nodded. "But we were interrupted by his doctor before we could discuss the matter further. Dad, why am I here? We could've discussed Castle business over the phone."

"It's more than that." His father motioned for Dro to stand so he could swing his legs over the side and get up. "Walk with me."

They left his mother tending to her roses while they strolled around the grounds.

"You haven't contacted Santiago yet."

It wasn't a question. Dro didn't like being reminded of things like he was still a child.

"I've been busy, Papa. Besides, we both know that Uncle Santiago has probably dug himself into another hole and just wants me to pay to bail him out."

"It's more complicated than that, *hijo*," he said in a weary tone. "He hasn't spoken to me about it in depth, but it's something about a deal he's trying to close."

"Oh, great," Dro muttered. He tried to hide his irritation, but it was hard. Though he hadn't said it aloud, he wondered how much of his uncle's shady business deals were what was putting a strain on his father's health. He'd tried to get his brothers, Christian and Esteban, to run interference with their uncle, but they'd both claimed to be too busy. Another fact that had annoyed him as of late. Neither of them was too busy when it came to their own interests.

"Alejandro," his father said in a firm voice. "He's family, and my brother. And we—"

"Never turn our back on each other," Dro finished for him.

"Qué pasa?"

Both men turned to see Esteban walking up behind them.

His father held up a hand to halt any further conversation.

"I don't know," Dro answered, taking in the upscale threads draping his brother's athletic frame. "How about you tell me what's up, and why you're always conveniently busy when I call?"

"Don't be dramatic." Esteban chuckled. He leaned in and clapped his brother on the back. Dro returned the gesture.

"*Mamá* told me you were here."

"Always the referee," Dro said under his breath.

His older brother fell into step. "So, what brings you home?"

"Business, what else?"

Esteban perked up. "What kind of business?"

"Nothing that you'd be interested in," Dro snapped back.

"Try me."

"*Silencio*," their father said tersely.

Both brothers clammed up. They continued walking without another word until reaching the pool deck. Victor returned to his seat and stretched out. He poured a fresh cup of tea before crossing his arms over his chest.

"*We* are supposed to look out for one another. Now that I'm no longer working, my responsibilities fall to my sons to continue with our family interests—all three of you. It saddens me that I have to keep reminding everyone."

"Of course, Papa," Esteban replied. "Being the oldest, the bulk of the responsibilities should fall to me."

Dro rolled his eyes at his brother's impassioned speech.

"I can work with Dro to turn over everything to—"

"You had the opportunity to step into my shoes before, Esteban," Victor snapped. "You refused. Alejandro is the only one of you that proved himself. I asked you to work with Khalil on some important Castle business, but you said that you couldn't leave your interests unattended."

"For good reason," Esteban countered. "The Castle is run by crooks now. Everyone knows that the King seats are in name only. There's no real prestige in being one anymore. Any power you all had is long gone."

His father's expression darkened. "Is that all that interests you, Esteban? Power? What about honor, and commitment to your brothers?"

"The Kings are your brothers, Papa. Not mine."

"That's enough," Victor roared, standing to his full height.

Valentina appeared out of nowhere. "*Mi amor*," she cautioned.

Instantly, Dro was at his father's side. He shot his brother a scathing glare. "You've gone too far."

"Forgive me," Esteban replied, backing down. "I meant no disrespect to you, Papa."

"To disrespect the legacy of the Castle *is* to disrespect me," Victor snapped. "You all are well aware of what The Castle was for. It is the main reason you live a life of luxury."

Their conversation was cut short by Laura's announcement that dinner was ready. During the meal, Esteban tried to smooth things over by talking about his wife and children. Victor enjoyed hearing about them and the tense moment between him and his son dissipated.

During dessert, Dro received a call. He glanced at his cell phone. Knowing how his mother felt about taking calls during a meal, he said, "I'm sorry, *Mamá*, but I have to take this."

She gave Dro a stern look but nodded.

Excusing himself, he stepped out and said, "Hi, hold on a minute."

He didn't speak again until he was in the sitting room down the hall.

"Sorry about that. What's up, Lola?"

"Do you normally place people on forget?"

He smiled. "It was a hold, not forget. My mother isn't a fan of having phones on during family mealtime. I know I'm going to hear about it later."

"Did you get the email I sent you?"

"No 'hi, how was your trip'?" he teased.

There was a slight pause before she said, "How was your trip, Dro?"

"Way too late," he teased. "And yes, I received your email, though I haven't had a chance to view it. Did you get mine?"

"Yes, and thank you. It was just what I needed," Lola replied. "Your associate is very thorough. It proves that the woman was trying to set Shawn up. It's obvious she was hoping to get a big payout by being caught with one of the Mayhews in a compromising position. Thanks to you, we can counter her claims that he didn't take no for an answer."

"Don't thank me. I did it for you, not Shawn Mayhew," he said, peering out the window at the lush landscape. "I don't care one bit if that waste of a human being gets taken to the cleaners for his indiscretions."

"You aren't going to like what you read," Lola cautioned.

Dro frowned. "Hang on."

He removed the phone from his ear and pulled up his email. He read Lola's document and almost bit his tongue to keep from letting out a string of expletives.

"This is bad."

"I know." When he didn't reply, she said, "What are you going to do, Dro?"

"Whatever I have to," he said between clenched teeth. "Because if my father finds out about this, it'll kill him."

CHAPTER 44

Grant was angry and trying to keep himself under control when he walked into Batter & Berries, one of Chicago's popular eateries. He immediately spotted the older, immaculately dressed man seated at a corner table holding court with four flawlessly dressed men. His command audience was closer to Grant's age, but it was clear that the older gentleman was their general.

He took a step forward but felt Meeks' hand grip his shoulder. Grant's instinct was to shake him off and plow ahead, but his beef was not with his friend.

Meeks dropped his hand. "Slow your roll. You can't go charging up to an alderman demanding answers without any proof of his involvement."

"Why the hell not?" Grant's brows puckered. "You were there when the call came in."

"Yes, but the caller only said that we were to meet with the man for more information. For all you know, the alderman could be an innocent bystander in this mess."

Grant looked over at Alderman James Knight and could see nothing innocent about the man. What he saw was an arrogant individual in his mid-fifties with a fake smile plastered on his round face. Grant saw through the façade and was ready to do battle with the general.

"He's no bystander. The man's an ass in a nice black suit."

Meeks' eyebrows rose and he looked down at the gray Armani suit he wore and the blue Giovanni suit Grant was sporting. "We're the ones wearing nice suits."

Grant's brows drew together. "You are *so* married. Let's go."

As the two approached the table, the four men stood in unison, offering the alderman a protective barrier as though he was The Don for a New York mob.

"Still think he's a bystander?" he whispered to Meeks while keeping his eyes on the men in his wake.

Before Grant could get the words past his lips, Meeks spoke up. "We're here to meet with Alderman Knight," he stated to no one in particular.

Grant shook his head. Meeks knew his friend could take care of himself, but he couldn't keep from slipping into a security role.

Alderman Knight rose slowly, and two men stepped to sandwich him. It was as if he'd parted the Red Sea.

"You must be Grant Khambrel," he stated, offering his hand.

Grant accepted his hand and replied, "That I am, and this is my business associate—"

"Meeks Montgomery," he supplied, holding out his hand. "Welcome to Chicago, gentlemen. Please, have a seat."

The alderman waved his hand, and three of the men vacated their seats, leaving the alderman alone with only one of his men. "Allow me to introduce you to my right-hand man, Richmond Banks." He offered a conspiratorial look and added, "And if my beautiful daughter finally smartens up, he'll be my future son-in-law."

Richmond smiled and shook both men's hands. "Come now, Alderman, we both know your daughter is exceptionally bright."

The older man's smile widened. "That she is," he proclaimed. "My pride and joy."

"Alderman, we appreciate you taking the time to meet with us," Grant said, sweeping aside all the small talk. "I have a problem. I've received a call directing me to you—"

Alderman Knight held up his hand, halting the conversation. He gestured for the waitress. "I'm old school gentleman, so we eat before any business gets conducted. This place is fantastic. May I recommend their famous French toast flight?"

The casual atmosphere and mouthwatering aroma reminded Grant of his favorite spot in Houston—the Breakfast Klub. He, too, often conducted business over a good meal. Unfortunately, he wasn't in the mood to be social. He frowned, and fisted his right hand on the table. Grant was a man who didn't like being told what to do.

"It's your city," Meeks stated, reaching for and silencing his vibrating phone.

Grant figured Meeks must have known he was about to blow a gasket and tell the good alderman what he could do with his French toast or any other flight. Refusing his offer would not only be rude; under the circumstances, it could cost him valuable information.

Alderman Knight grinned. "Nice. It usually takes people a lot longer to realize that fact."

The waitress took their orders, but not before fawning all over the alderman. Grant could admit the man was handsome and well-built for any age, but his attitude that irritated him the most. As if the woman's behavior was expected versus appreciated.

Their food was delivered in record time, but they could barely get through the meal without someone stopping by to pay homage to the self-proclaimed king. While Grant found everything to be tasty, he was done being cordial. For all he knew, the alderman could be the one behind the blackmail. He had questions that needed answers, so pushing past his distaste was paramount. Grant pushed his plate aside and leaned back in the chair. Meeks copied the movement.

"Alderman Knight, while I appreciate the hospitality and this great meal, I think it's time we get to the reason for our visit."

"Business ... important business," Meeks chimed in.

The alderman used a cloth napkin to wipe his mouth before reaching for a glass of juice. After draining the glass, he called for the teenage busboy to remove the dirty dishes.

"Now, what business might that be?" He sat back in the chair and folded his arms across a barrel chest. "Richmond, do you have any idea what business we might have with these men?"

"No sir, I don't," he replied, giving Grant a disdainful onceover.

Grant was starting to lose his patience with the games these two were playing. "Look—"

"Could it be that you *unlawfully* submitted a proposal and won the United Center contract perhaps?" Alderman Knight ran the back of his hand under a chin that couldn't decide if it wanted to be a single or a double.

"There was nothing unlawful about our submission and something tells me you know that too," Grant countered.

"The only thing I know is that you submitted a bid without disclosing your prior relationship with the Wirtz Company."

"That's not true—"

"And after winning said bid, your duplicity was discovered, and now you need help getting out of this mess," the alderman stated in a matter-of-fact tone.

"Help that only you can provide, I assume," Meeks stated, locking an intense glare on the older man.

"How much is that *help* going to cost me?" Grant asked, trying to control his temper.

"Not one penny," Alderman Knight replied, grinning in that patronizing way that set Grant's teeth on edge.

Grant suddenly felt sick to the stomach, wondering just how much of his life was about to implode.

"That's how we do things here in Chicago," Richmond said, leaning forward. "You help us ... and we help you."

"How?" Grant and Meeks chorused.

"I sit on the committee that led the search for the architect and construction company that will expand the United Center," Richmond started to explain. "I'm also the person who found the error in your proposal, so it's only right that I correct things. I'll graciously fall on my sword, admit my mistake and all will be well."

"That's my boy," Alderman Knight praised, obviously proud of the man he was grooming.

"I'm a busy man. Things have been a little hectic lately," Richmond ventured. "Between business and trying to win my woman's hand—"

"No worries, my daughter will come around. I promise you that," the alderman assured.

Grant couldn't believe this older man was talking about his daughter as if she was a prize horse to be bartered. For a brief moment, the stunning mystery woman from the hospital filled into Grant's mind, and his body responded. He fought back the unexpected desire, but deep down he realized that last look she gave him was something to explored. The puppy sitting next to the alderman was about to lose out big time.

Alderman Knight whipped out his cell and swiped until he came to a particular photo. "Lovely, isn't she? Now you see why Richmond is losing his mind, eh?"

Grant froze. The image on the screen was of the mysterious woman he had seen in the hospital on his visit to Khalil a few days ago. The woman who captured his attention in one instant. What were the odds?

His gaze met Meeks', and he realized his friend and business associate was about five minutes away from making this a very bad day for everyone.

"Look, things can slip through the cracks … get misplaced. Only a handful of people know about the assumed mistake, and nothing's been released publicly. Once I 'fix' the error," he used air quotes to make his point. "Everything will move forward with no blemishes to your name or reputation."

He doesn't have everything. He doesn't know the whole story. Who's pulling the alderman's strings?

"For now," Alderman Knight said before his expression hardened. "We come to an agreement, and you get to work turning the United Center into a showcase this city can be proud of for years to come."

"And if we can't come to terms?" Meeks asked, his face twisted in anger.

"Then your friend over there can kiss five hundred million dollars in profit goodbye. Which I believe," he tilted his head slightly to the left. "A nice chunk of which goes into the already flush coffers of Blake and Montgomery."

"This is a win-win for us all, gentlemen," Richmond said, reaching for his glass of water. "Like I said, you help us, we help you."

"And exactly what type of help are you looking for?" Meeks asked, clenching his jaw.

The old man leaned back in his chair, held Grant's gaze, and replied, "Access. All we want is a little access."

Grant grimaced and asked, "To what, exactly?"

Alderman Knight sneered, "That precious Castle you all seem to revere so damn much."

CHAPTER 45

The sun's rays beaming through the moon roof didn't lend any relief to the weight of Kaleb's thoughts as he drifted from Lake Shore Drive onto Columbus then pulled over in front of one of his favorite childhood hangouts. Kaleb easily found a parking space in the traffic-packed area in front of Buckingham Fountain.

"Call Zephyr," he demanded of Siri as though she were human.

"Wassup, cousin?" Zephyr answered in his usual cheerful voice. "Well, Prodigal Cousin. Seems as much as you didn't want to go to Chicago by private jet, you and it love the Windy City a lot more than you thought. I haven't heard a peep from either one since you landed. Weren't you supposed to be back in Detroit like ... oh ... three days ago?"

"Hey, Z," Kaleb said, tension coloring his tone. "I've been rolling with the punches because the punches keep rolling in." A dull ache radiated in the front of Kaleb's head as he prepared to share his current circumstances with Zephyr—he'd never had to make this type of call to his cousin.

"What's the problem?" Zephyr laughed. "You only left a few days ago, man. There shouldn't have been anything requiring that tone of voice."

"This is serious, Z," Kaleb chastised. "You know the property in Auburn Gresham we were discussing before I left?"

"Yeah," Zephyr responded. Silence stretched between them as the gravity of Kaleb's tone settled in Zephyr's mind.

"I kinda need to hang out in Chicago while they investigate a suspicious fire."

"Are you being charged?" Zephyr asked, his voice escalating with the news.

"No, not yet, but it gets worse."

"How so?"

Kaleb adjusted the seat of his car as he sat in silence. Watching the people amble along the sidewalk in front of the fountain, he hesitated to share the events and discoveries of his short time in the city with the man he considered his brother. Even though Zephyr was younger, Kaleb always admired Zephyr's ambition, his generosity, and his heart for people.

"There are bodies attached to the property. Five girls that were reported as missing died in the fire and the detective on the case ..." Kaleb swallowed past the lump in his throat, his heart filling with sadness over such young lives cut short, and in such an ugly way. "I remember him always being posted at the corner store in my neighborhood with his buddy. His partner is the one who collared my boys on that bogus gang rape charge that got me and mom caught up. I wasn't anywhere near that party, or the girl that night."

"You're talking too much," Zephyr warned. "Is your phone being tapped?"

"I gave them my name and occupation. It would be easy to find me."

"Get a burner after you call a lawyer."

"I made contact with Rock already. He'll be here Monday to go over the case."

"How long do they foresee this investigation taking?" Zephyr asked, and his voice held more than concern. "Do you have anyone to take care of your business here?"

Kaleb pinched his nose and released a gust of air as he chastised himself for not having someone he trusted enough to run his business in case of an emergency. Zephyr was always a willing investment partner if the dollars made sense, but had his own business to run. Unfortunately, Kaleb didn't trust anyone else—a direct side effect of traumatic events and losses from his childhood, and more recently, Meme Rogers.

"Not officially," Kaleb sighed. "Every person I thought I could trust had some issue going on and I just never got around to promoting anyone."

"And you're sure MeMe can't hold ground for a minute?"

"Like I told you, we parted ways a year ago," Kaleb revealed as he lowered the car windows to catch the breeze from Lake Michigan. During their long-term relationship, MeMe Rogers had also made the mistake of becoming a little too close with one of Kaleb's competitors and her explanations weren't adding up and neither was the fact that his competitor seemed to have the jump on some deals no one was supposed to know about.

"Wait a minute," Zephyr said. "You mentioned a woman named Skyler earlier. Isn't that Reno's right-hand woman? He's going to shit a brick."

"Well, there's more to her than being his right hand," he shot back. "We'll have a chance to talk about my love life later. What I need now is someone *you* trust that can run my business for a few weeks."

No sooner than Kaleb made his request, he spotted a familiar face two cars away that sent a chill down his back. Narrowing his gaze, he stared at what he hoped was an illusion.

"I've got you, K," Zephyr declared. "Run down the layout of the operation so I can get my man started as soon as possible ...." Zephyr's voice trailed off as Kaleb's attention shifted to a black-and-red-cloaked figure that stood in front of the lush green manicured bushes separating the bustling park from Columbus Drive. "K, did you hear me? I said I've got you."

Shadow.

The Lake Michigan breeze was no contest for the heat that rose up Kaleb's back as the man sneered in his direction.

How is Chicago not large enough for me to stay out of sight from these people? I'm not back in the city five damn seconds. Now they're finding me like I never left.

Kaleb's nostrils flared as wide as tunnels as he thought of the last time he saw Shadow's face. He sported the same gold-capped front teeth and gang symbol of The ChiTown Hellions tattooed on his neck. The identification was unmistakable.

A single hot tear trailed down Kaleb's chiseled cheek as memories of his father flashed through his mind. The man who was a gentle giant to him and his mother died in his arms, pooled in blood from the multiple gunshot wounds he sustained in a drive-by shooting outside of their family home. Shadow had a face that Kaleb would never forget.

"KV," Zephyr yelled from the phone, breaking Kaleb's focus on the tall, slender man who stared him down as he crossed the busy avenue.

"Yeah," Kaleb responded, not realizing Zephyr had been calling his name for the better part of a whole minute.

"Where'd you go?"

"Do you remember me ever talking about my mentor, Khalil Germaine?" Kaleb asked, not answering the question, but keeping his sights on Shadow, who weaved his way through a crowd of people that didn't have the height to hide him.

"Vaguely."

"Well, there's a situation with him, but I can't talk about it right now," Kaleb explained. "I'm not comfortable leaving the state because the police have their eyes on me. His family residence is the only place I think is safe to stay until all of this clears up. You can have the pilot veer the jet back to Detroit and I'll call you when I get that burner."

"Is Aunt Rosa safe?"

"She's in Schaumburg, totally unaware that an extended vacation is in her near future while Rock and I work on the case. I'll let you know the plans once I get settled."

"Okay. I'll put my guy Derrick Winfree over your operations. He's excellent with management and numbers," Zephyr assured his cousin. "Email me details, text me the passwords separately and I'll match them with what's in the email. Then send an explanation for your employees and any other pertinent information as soon as possible."

CHAPTER 46

Vikkas had fantasized about being alone with Milan for thirteen years. Now that they were, with no other distractions and no buffers of friends and family, his castle had never appeared so small and plain. That was the effect Milan had on him. Her mere presence made everything seem so intimately significant, as if each moment in time had been specially carved into the stars just so they could exist within that space together, sharing the same breath.

He would not be considered a meek and feeble man by any stretch of the imagination, yet suddenly, a nervous energy roiled within him, making his mouth parch and his palms go sweaty. *What the hell?*

Vikkas had to get it together. He had dreamt of the uncharted possibilities that had lived only in the grayscale of his dreams. Finally, he had the opportunity to light them up in brilliant, vivid color.

"How about a drink?" he suggested, if only to cut the awkwardness of expectation.

Milan nodded. "That would be great."

Vikkas poured her a glass of Stella Rosa Platinum and she took a long, comforting sip, wondering how he knew that it was her favorite. It had been a day, to say the least. Milan was exhausted, but being here with Vikkas in his gorgeous, elaborate home had energized her. Never in a million years did she think she'd be in a castle—*his* castle, no less.

But the true fairytale was being with him after all these years. Even time could not suppress the fire that still burned hot between them. If anything, seeing him so fiercely defend and protect her only made the blaze rage even brighter.

Without another word, Vikkas grasped Milan's hand, intertwining their fingers, and led her down a long, maze-like corridor. They passed room after room until coming to stop at a set of intricately carved dark wood doors. Milan looked up at Vikkas, brows furrowed.

"Um, this doesn't look like the kitchen," she mused, taking in the area that was far away from the luxurious quarters where she had settled.

"Because it's not," he replied. No humor in his tone, it was all warmth. "My room."

"Oh." Her mouth went dry.

"I thought you might want to venture out a little. My father's been taking up way too much of your time."

"Can I help it that he loves me?" she teased, giving him a sly smile.

"No, I understand completely, because I can't help it that I love you."

She gasped as Vikkas gripped a curved handle and pressed down to click open the door. "There's something I want to show you here so you'll understand what I feel for you has never gone away."

Milan followed Vikkas into the room only to stop short just two feet inside, her mouth ajar and wide-eyed gaze filled with awe. Every wall was graced with the most beautiful artwork she had ever seen. Pieces that rivaled collections in the country's most famed galleries had found their home right here in his bedroom. And they all had one characteristic in common: they were all of Black women. Black women that, coincidentally, favored her.

"Where did you find all these?" she gasped.

"I've been collecting for a while now. At first, it was just a couple pieces, but then I realized … I was searching for something. Or someone."

Milan turned to face Vikkas and his sultry dark eyes seemed to pierce right through to her heart. His stare was intense and hungry, and it would have scared her had she not been warring with her own inner craving.

"What are you looking at?" she asked, her voice trembling with anticipation.

Vikkas wet his bottom lip with the tip of his tongue before answering, "Art."

Before she could suck in a steadying breath, his large hand was tightening his grip on her back and pulling her frame into his. The second their mouths collided, they both moaned, releasing years of relinquished heartache, yearning, and all-consuming love they had denied.

He could not get enough of the taste of Milan's tongue sliding against his. He could kiss her like this every day for the rest of his life—and he planned to. He would not tire of her lips or the way they seemed to melt into his so seamlessly, as if they were created only for him to devour. He needed to have more of her. Needed to sate the wild hunger that seemed to grow every time her breasts brushed against his chest. He could feel her pebbled nipples through the ivory blouse. And now he had to taste them.

His hands dipped lower to grasp her luscious, round backside and he squeezed, lifting her right off her feet with ease. She squealed but he refused to stop kissing her. He would swallow all her mewls of delight tonight. Every. Single. One.

Milan did not hesitate to wrap her legs around his waist. She could feel him pulsing between their ravenous bodies, thickening with every step towards the four-poster king-sized bed. He laid her down gently and she couldn't help but squirm at the loss of contact when he stood upright to gaze down at her. She was panting with desire at the way his eyes roamed her body, as though committing every single curve to memory. It was driving her mad.

"I want you," she could barely get out.

"And you will have me. All of me."

Vikkas started with the buttons of his shirt, slowly unfastening each one with deft fingers. Once the fabric slid from his shoulders and onto the floor, revealing chiseled mounds of olive skin, Milan couldn't hold back anymore. She sat up, eager to touch the taut ripples of his abs and chest. His body was magnificent, just as she had imagined. And she couldn't wait to feel him in every way.

He grabbed the hem of Milan's blouse and stripped it from her torso. She had always taken care of herself, so he wasn't surprised to find that she had on a black lace bra that perfectly accentuated her full breasts. As sexy as it was on her, he couldn't deny himself the pleasure of unsnapping it so he could hold those heavy mounds in his palms. She moaned loudly as he massaged and rolled his thumbs over the nipples. Dammit, he needed them in his mouth— *now*.

In one swift motion, he gently pushed her back down and covered one with his mouth. Then he tasted the other, sending Milan into a frenzy. But he wasn't done with her yet. While his tongue licked and sucked, his hands worked on sliding her pants down over her hips and thighs. Her sweet breasts weren't the only part of her he'd taste tonight.

Milan felt dizzy with pleasure as Vikkas kissed a trail down her body, only stopping at the delta of heat that literally ached for him. The first touch was his fingers, parting her slick, silky folds. He placed the fingers in his mouth to sample her.

"You're so sweet," he rasped. "I'm going to drink every ounce of you."

His words were so erotic that Milan thought she might explode with the first flick of his tongue over her pearl. But she didn't. She came with the third. And it was so hard and devastating that her back arched off the bed. She couldn't even scream. But Vikkas didn't stop there.

Vikkas made good on his threat and sucked and licked every drop of her release with appreciative groans that sent vibrations to her already hypersensitive sex. If this was so good she wanted to cry, how could she handle any more? How could she survive his hardness filling her to the brim and stroking deep and long? They had never expressed this facet of their love before, although she had spent many nights fantasizing about it. Now Vikkas would mark more than just her heart. He would mark her soul.

Milan watched intently as Vikkas unfastened his pants and let them fall to the floor. He was splendid; every thick inch was perfectly sculpted and smooth, like silk over steel. She wanted to reach out and touch him, but the need to have Vikkas between her thighs was far too great. He wasted no time spreading her wide and teasing the trembling flesh with his tip. Then Vikkas entered her slowly, letting her body stretch to accommodate his size.

She cried out as each inch provided a new level of ecstasy. Pain … pleasure … each sensation melded into the next until she couldn't tell where his body began and where hers ended. They became one. And as he thrust into her, touching the deepest, warmest parts of her soul, she knew that nothing on earth would ever tear them apart again.

Vikkas could have never imagined how good it would be with Milan. She was tight, yet her body molded to him like she was designed especially for him. She was so wet and hot that he was at risk of losing control, but he'd be damned if he didn't make this last. He had waited far too long to finally make love to her. This may not have been his first time but hell, it felt like it. But it also felt like forever.

He slowed the movements of his hips and covered Milan's shivering frame with his. He held her tightly and kissed her deeply, keeping perfectly in time with his strokes. When he lifted his head, he noticed that there were tears streaming down the sides of her face.

"Baby, what's wrong?"

Milan shook her head. "Nothing is wrong. Everything is so right. Finally, everything is the way it should be."

Vikkas kissed away the salty rivulets of emotion, murmuring his heart's song against her humid skin. He understood the overwhelming rush of passion. He, too, felt like he had waited entire lifetimes to commit himself to Milan—mind, body, and soul. And he vowed right then and there, as he scorched her womb with his promise, that he would never let anything or anyone take her from him again.

CHAPTER 47

The empty chair at the round table struck an ominous note. Several of the men occasionally looked at the vacant seat, as though Dwayne would somehow mysteriously appear.

"We will fill it with someone who fits with our purpose and vibe," Vikkas said, though he also felt the weight of Dwayne's absence. "Like King Arthur's roundtable, we too are all equals here. My family connection to the founder has no bearing. I just want to say that."

Daron slid to the edge of his seat. "By the way, I received a call from a Nayan Maharaj …"

Vikkas visibly stiffened at hearing that name and a few men at the table peered at him curiously as he tried to hold in his anger.

"He requested an audience—his words, an audience," Daron said. "He mentioned something about knowing information about my past."

"Same here," Grant said, looking at Jai. "What's his deal? Is he related to you?"

"He called me as well," Reno said before Jai could answer.

"Me too," Kaleb chimed in as Shaz nodded, affirming that he had also received that mysterious call.

"I'll get into it," Daron said, sliding back into a more comfortable position in his chair.

"Don't bother," Vikkas warned. "He's a nuisance looking for a way to get at The Castle's money since he has none. He did not want any of you to have a stake because he feels it was started with Maharaj funds and now should return into the family fold. They meant The Castle's money, not my father."

"And not you," Dro challenged, a steely gaze on Vikkas.

"I would have been given a restoration to the Maharaj family name," Vikkas confessed, taking a long, slow breath to center himself. "But that is not my priority. This is. It's why I'm here ..." He swept an intense gaze across each of them. "With you, my brothers. United in a purpose that serves more than just ourselves."

Daron adjusted his hat and a small smile played about the corners of his lips. "Like I said, I'll get into it."

"Let's dispense with any naysayers at this point," Shaz said, sliding a package of legal documents and stock certificates in front of each member and one at the empty spot that should have been held by Dwayne. "Sign this paperwork and we're all in."

Vikkas placed a silver passkey on top. One that mirrored the kind that had been given to Kaleb a few days ago. Each one of the men took a moment to observe the card and what it meant—keys to the Kingdom.

"I have a favor to ask of each of you," Vikkas said.

"Again?" Jai said, feigning frustration and giving him the side-eye. "I think you're all out of those, my brother."

"Not that kind of favor," Vikkas confirmed as the other men shared a laugh at his expense. "I'd like each of you to stand up with me at my wedding to Milan. My father spoke with her to ensure that being with me was in line with what she wanted. He gave his blessing."

"That's what's up," Kaleb said and a round of applause and congratulations followed.

When their voices died down, Reno stood and said, "We need to read our new designations and appointment aloud to make it more of a vow and not just words on paper." He gestured to the documents and said, "I am King of Chatham, and I will be responsible for rescuing the trafficking victims that were illegally filtered through The Castle. I will also work with Daron on finding missing women and children."

Grant flipped a file open to the first page, stood, and grinned. "I am King of Lincoln Park, and I will be responsible for untangling The Castle's properties from any illegal deals they may now be mired in, as well as purchasing new lands and properties worldwide to further the purpose of The Castle."

Jai stood and without opening the folder, said, "I am King of Devon, and I will be responsible for the health and well-being of The Castle, its Kings, and the holistic center that Khalil founded on the grounds."

Daron rose and declared, "I am King of Morgan Park, and I will be responsible for vetting members, contractors, security systems at The Castle, as well as security for Khalil and all of the Kings and their families."

Dro tapped an index finger on the folder. "I am King of Hyde Park, and I am responsible for any special assignments that Khalil or any man here may give me."

"Well, that's a little vague," Kaleb said, frowning.

"It's supposed to be," Dro countered. "Sometimes you all will need plausible deniability."

"Well, why do we—"

"Kaleb," Shaz said, getting to his feet and slamming a hand on the table in front of Kaleb. "Leave it be. With Dro, we are on a need to know basis. Right now, we don't need to know."

Dro gave him a grateful nod. Kaleb squared his shoulders and remained silent.

"Since I'm already standing," Shaz continued. "I am King of Evanston and I will be responsible for all legal documents and systems put in place for The Castle. I will also go over every document the previous members signed and see exactly how to extricate The Castle from anything that might be considered not in our best interest."

Vikkas, who was now on his feet, looked toward Kaleb, who gestured that he should take the floor.

"I am King of Wilmette," Vikkas said. "I will be responsible for the international holdings of The Castle as well as all intellectual property therein."

"Therein?" Kaleb teased. "Legalese even when it's informal."

Vikkas grinned and shrugged. "You know, what can I say? I *am* a lawyer."

Kaleb sighed, stood, and looked to all the men around him. "I am King of South Shore and I will be responsible for development projects in underprivileged neighborhoods in Chicago."

The men had a toast to their new assignments.

"I always wanted to be part of his message," Vikkas confessed. "But right here with you is where I belong. Khalil has said what we are to do is the most important work ever."

Each of them swore an oath to protect The Castle and each other from anyone that would do them harm. They had failed to answer the call the first time and darkness had invaded The Castle, threatening their way of life and the very heart of their city. Evil had been allowed to permeate, but with their efforts, it would spread no further.

The Kings of the Castle would take back what was theirs and claim their place as their mentor had intended. They would fight for their way of life, and the city they all loved dearly. Not just for Khalil, but for each other. Then each of them vowed to do whatever it took to avenge their mentor.

"Now, for my part in things," Daron said, reaching into his pocket and whipping out nine pairs of single diamond studs. "I'd like for each of you to wear these."

"I hate to be the one to tell you, but they're not my color," Jai said.

"My ears aren't pierced, but it's a lovely thought," Reno teased. "Next time, try flowers."

A round of laughter echoed before Daron said, "Each one of them are high frequency tracking devices. One for you, and one for your beloved—if you have one."

That admission brought complete silence.

"Why would we need those?" Jai asked.

"Isn't it obvious?" Daron said. "We just signed paperwork that puts us in line with more money than even millionaires see in a lifetime, and you don't think you'll become targets? We already have the old guard

Castle members coming at us. This right here will mean that I'm able to find you even when your enemies think they have the upper hand."

"That's fine and all," Dro said, fingering the device as Kaleb replaced the one stud he was wearing with Daron's tech. Grant and Vikkas did the same. "But I'm not wearing an earring. An ass whipping and near-death experience is worth not having to explain to my parents why I suddenly have an earring at thirty-two years old." He gave Daron a basic head nod. "Brother, you're the technical genius. Find another way."

Daron sighed, closed his eyes for a moment. The rapid movements under his eyelids signaled his thought process. "Tattoos." His eyes flew open. "The only other way I can make something a part of you that can't be lost or taken off is a small tattoo on the inner part of your wrist."

Jai and Vikkas shared a look with Dro, who nodded his appreciation of the new plan.

Daron rounded the table, walking a path behind them. "If you're in distress, you might not get the opportunity to put your wrist to your heart to activate it. However, we can do a tattoo on the inside of the wrist that would have to be pressed for at least ten seconds. That way if you're tied up, it can be easily activated by pressing the wrist to the closest object."

"Do you always think in worst case scenarios?" Jai asked, reaching into his pocket to check his cell.

"It's what I've done for the majority of my life," he said, and Dro held out his fist for a pound. Daron smiled, then obliged.

"Speaking of worst-case scenarios ..." Jai grimaced. "We need to wrap this up. I have another emergency."

"We need to put up another fifty grand?" Shaz teased.

"No," Jai answered. "Looks like my comatose patient—*pregnant* comatose patient—is experiencing some distress."

"That sounds deep," Reno said. "How did it happen?"

"That's what the police are trying to figure out at this very moment," Jai said.

"Let me know if you need my help," Shaz said.

Daron tapped Dro's shoulder. "The tattoo will pulse for a few seconds so if it's accidentally turned on, it can be quickly turned off. Will that work for you?"

"Most definitely," Dro said, and the others chimed in before sliding the earrings back his way. "See, I told you all this man is a genius."

"That's pouring it on a little thick for a man who's scared of his Mama," Kaleb said, causing the others to chuckle.

"Show of hands of any man in this house who doesn't have a healthy fear of the number one woman in your lives."

Not a single hand went up.

"Thought so," Dro taunted, and settled back into the seat.

Daron dropped the earrings into the palm of his hand. "But I offer that you can keep these to give to the most important people in your life. Just let me know their names so I can put it in our system. The device will be connected to that person from this point on."

Vikkas held up the silver passkey. "You each have assigned quarters in The Castle, named for the place you once resided. Devon, South Shore, Hyde Park, Lincoln Park, Morgan Park, Evanston, Wilmette, and—"

"Lawndale," Dwayne supplied, and everyone turned to the man at the entrance wearing a black suit, silver tie, and a megawatt smile.

The men all left the table, some rushing to embrace Dwayne as he said, "You know what they say, better late than never."

The projection screen on the far end of the boardroom flickered on, and Khalil's face appeared. "And my saying has always been that it is better to never be late." He shifted in the hospital bed as his smile struggled to fall into place. "What took you so long?"

ABOUT THE KINGS OF THE CASTLE SERIES

Books 2-9 are standalones, no cliffhangers, and can be read in any order.

Book 1 – Kings of the Castle, the introduction to the series and story of King of Wilmette (Vikkas Germaine)

USA TODAY, New York Times, and National Bestselling Authors work together to provide you with a world you'll never want to leave. The Castle. Powerful men unexpectedly brought together by their pasts and current circumstances will become a force to be reckoned with. Their combined efforts to find the people responsible for the attempt on their mentor's life, is the beginning of dangerous challenges that will alter the path of their lives forever. Not to mention, they will also draw the ire and deadly intent of current Castle members who wield major influence across the globe.

Fate made them brothers, but protecting the Castle and the women they love, will make them Kings.

www.thekingsofthecastle.com

King of Chatham - Book 2

While Mariano "Reno" DeLuca uses his skills and resources to create safe havens for battered women, a surge in criminal activity within the Chatham area threatens the women's anonymity and security. When Zuri, an exotic Tanzanian Princess, arrives seeking refuge from an arranged marriage and its deadly consequences, Reno is now forced to relocate the women in the shelter, fend off unforeseen enemies of The Castle, and endeavor not to lose his heart to the mysterious woman.

King of Evanston - Book 3

Raised as an immigrant, he knows the heartache of family separation firsthand. His personal goals and business ethics collide when a vulnerable woman stands to lose her baby in an underhanded and profitable scheme crafted by powerful, ruthless businessmen and politicians who have nefarious ties to The Castle. Shaz and the Kings of the Castle collaborate to uproot the dark forces intent on changing the balance of power within The Castle and destroying their mentor. National Bestselling Author, J.L. Campbell presents book 3 in the Kings of the Castle Series, featuring Shaz Bostwick.

King of Devon - Book 4

When a coma patient becomes pregnant, Jaidev Maharaj's medical facility comes under a government microscope and media scrutiny. In the midst of the investigation, he receives a mysterious call from someone in his past that demands that more of him than he's ever been willing to give and is made aware of a dark family secret that will destroy the people he loves most.

King of Morgan Park - Book 5

Two things threaten to destroy several areas of Daron Kincaid's life— the tracking device he developed to locate victims of sex trafficking and an inherited membership in a mysterious outfit called The Castle. The new developments set the stage to dismantle the relationship with a woman who's been trained to make men weak or put them on the other side of the grave. The secrets Daron keeps from Cameron and his inner circle only complicates an already tumultuous situation caused by an FBI sting that brought down his former enemies. Can Daron take on his enemies, manage his secrets and loyalty to the Castle without permanently losing the woman he loves?

King of South Shore - Book 6

Award-winning real estate developer, Kaleb Valentine, is known for turning failing communities into thriving havens in the Metro Detroit area. His plans to rebuild his hometown neighborhood are dereailed with one phone call that puts Kaleb deep in the middle of an intense criminal investigation led by a detective who has a personal vendetta. Now he will have to deal with the ghosts of his past before they kill him.

King of Lincoln Park - Book 7

Grant Khambrel is a sexy, successful architect with big plans to expand his Texas Company. Unfortunately, a dark secret from his past could destroy it all unless he's willing to betray the man responsible for that success, and the woman who becomes the key to his salvation.

King of Hyde Park - Book 8

Alejandro "Dro" Reyes has been a "fixer" for as long as he could remember, which makes owning a crisis management company focused on repairing professional reputations the perfect fit. The same could be said of Lola Samuels, who is only vaguely aware of his "true" talents and seems to be oblivious to the growing attraction between them. His company, Vantage Point, is in high demand and business in the Windy City is booming. Until a mysterious call following an attempt on his mentor's life forces him to drop everything and accept a fated position with The Castle. But there's a hidden agenda and unexpected enemy that Alejandro doesn't see coming who threatens his life, his woman, and his throne.

King of Lawndale - Book 9

Dwayne Harper's passion is giving disadvantaged boys the tools to transform themselves into successful men. Unfortunately, the minute he steps up to take his place among the men he considers brothers, two things stand in his way: a political office that does not want the competition Dwayne's new education system will bring, and a well-connected former member of The Castle who will use everything in his power—even those who Dwayne mentors—to shut him down.

AUTHOR BIOS

Naleighna Kai is the *USA TODAY* Bestselling Author of Every Woman Needs a Wife, Open Door Marriage, Loving Me for Me, Slaves of Heaven and several other controversial novels. She is founder of NK Tribe Called Success, The Cavalcade of Authors, and is a publishing and marketing consultant. www.naleighnakai.com

S. L. Jennings is a military wife, mom of three, coffee addict, Willy Wonka enthusiast, and real-life unicorn. She's also the New York Times and USA Today Bestselling author of Taint, Fear of Falling and the Se7en Sinners Series, along with a few other titles that she's too lazy to type. She's been with her high school sweetheart for almost twenty years, and he still can't get her Subway sandwich order right. But he's cute and brings her vodka, so she keeps him around. They currently reside in Spokane, WA with their three stinky boys and their equally stinky cat. www.sljenningsauthor.com

Martha Kennerson is the bestselling and award-winning author who's love of reading and writing is a significant part of who she is. She uses both to create the kinds of stories that touch the heart. Martha lives with her family in League City, Texas. She believes her current blessings are only matched by the struggle it took to achieve such happiness. To find out more about Martha and her journey, visit her website at www.marthakennerson.com and you can follow her on Facebook and Twitter.

J. L. Campbell is an award-winning Jamaican author who has written over thirty books in several romance subgenres. Campbell, who features Jamaican culture in her stories, is a certified editor, and also writes non-fiction. Visit her on the web at www.joylcampbell.com.

National bestselling author, **Lisa Watson**, is a native of Washington D.C., and writes in the Multicultural & Interracial, Contemporary, Romantic Suspense, and Sweet Romance genres. Her memorable novels for the Harlequin's Kimani line, The Match Broker series was listed as one of 2014's Top 25 Books of the Summer, and Top 50 Best Reads. Lisa lives in Raleigh, North Carolina with her husband of twenty-two years and two teenagers, and is avidly working on book one, Alexa King: The Guardian, in her second new Romantic Suspense series, The Lady Doyen and Book 2 in the Love and Danger Series. www.lisawatson.com

Karen D. Bradley is a national bestselling author and screenplay writer. English and Grammar were never her strongest subjects, but as life would have it, her weakest link would become her saving grace. Writing fiction became one of her favorite forms of therapy. She has penned several contemporary fiction, suspense, and romantic suspense novels. Visit Karen on the web at www.karendbradley.com

Janice M. Allen is a National Bestselling Author who has always been an avid reader of fiction. She even edited the work of other authors for several years. But she gets an incomparable thrill from creating stories that entertain readers and cause them to reflect on real life issues. No Right Way To Do A Wrong Thing is her first novel, followed by her short story Cayenne. www.janicemallen.com

London St. Charles has always had a passion for the pen, paper, and books. She is a Chicago native who uses the Windy City as a backdrop to the romance, suspense, and contemporary fiction stories she writes. London published her debut novel, The Husband We Share in 2017 and is one of nine authors in the anthology, Sugar. She also composes an online newsletter, London Writes, that keeps readers abreast of what's going on in her world. www.londonstcharles.com

MarZe Scott is a lifelong resident of Ypsilanti, Michigan and Graduate of University of Michigan. A lover of all things creative, MarZé enjoys reading, free-hand illustrating, jewelry making and makeup artistry.

Known for her vivid and captivating storytelling, MarZé has been writing short stories and poems since elementary school and developed a taste in high school for writing about provocative topics like the consequences of casual sex. You can find Gemini Rising, MarZé's debut novel, and short story Next Lifetime wherever books are sold. www.marzescott.com

SERIES MENTORS:

LaVerne Thompson is a *USA Today* Bestselling, award winning, multi-published author, an avid reader and a writer of contemporary, fantasy, and sci/fi sensual romances. She loves creating worlds within and without our world. She also writes romantic suspense and new adult romance under the pen name Ursula Sinclair also a USA Today Bestselling Author. www.lavernethompson.com

Kassanna is a strong believer in love at first sight and happily ever afters. Writing has always been her passion but fate sometimes has other roads that must first be taken .Navigating the road less traveled was not only unexpected but in the end extremely rewarding. Her books are mainly contemporary romance but she has delved into the paranormal, fantasy, and plans on expanding into other areas as the ideas come to her. Right now she is enjoying life and seeing her works come into fruition make it that much more pleasurable especially when her books make others smile. Kassanna wouldn't have it any other way. www.flavorfullove.com